13

W9-BAR-228

"Having fun?"

"The best." Melanie squinted into the sun.

"I'm glad." Gabe was glad to see her smile. "This tree swing has quite the reputation around here."

"Oh, really? What does it do?"

Gabe stared into the most incredibly blue eyes he'd ever seen. A blush from the sun settled on her cheeks and a smattering of light freckles dusted over her nose. He swallowed and tried to find his voice. "It makes people throw caution to the wind."

A light sparked in her eye and he thought he saw her wink. "Me? Throw caution to the wind? Not in a million years."

Gabe offered Melanie a hand up. Her fingers were warm in his palm. They locked gazes and couldn't look away. His insides churned.

Then her son Jason ran up and wrapped his arms around her. "You were great!" He turned toward Gabe. "Will you push me, Gabe?"

Gabe nodded. Melanie looked away, breaking the spell between them. She ruffled Jason's hair.

"Okay. Just once." She glanced back again with a shy smile. "Then my turn."

All Gabe could do was nod.

AUDRA HARDERS

moved to Colorado when she was nine years old and sees no reason to leave the state she loves. Her parents held out as long as they could, but eventually bought a horse for her when she was in seventh grade. Didn't matter that she was allergic to everything under the sun, especially horses. She'd feed, brush and ride that horse until the sneezing and itching drove her to the showers. Today you'll find her undergoing allergy shots so she can enjoy all the wonders living in Colorado offers—including riding horses without sneezing.

In fourth grade, she met the most obnoxious little boy in Sunday school—he ended up becoming the love of her life. Talk about overcoming conflict! They've been married more than twenty years and she can't imagine life without her best friend. They have two grown children, and share their Front Range home with three dogs, various sheep, goats, chickens, a fifteen-pound rabbit and a guard turkey.

Rocky Mountain Hero

Audra Harders

Published by Steeple Hill Books™

If you purchased this book without a cover you should be aware that this book is stolen property. It was reported as "unsold and destroyed" to the publisher, and neither the author nor the publisher has received any payment for this "stripped book."

STEEPLE HILL BOOKS

PLEASE RECYCLE • THIS PRODUCT IS RECYCLABLE •
Recycling programs for this product may not exist in your area.

ISBN-13: 978-0-373-87648-8

ROCKY MOUNTAIN HERO

Copyright © 2011 by Audra Harders

All rights reserved. Except for use in any review, the reproduction or utilization of this work in whole or in part in any form by any electronic, mechanical or other means, now known or hereafter invented, including xerography, photocopying and recording, or in any information storage or retrieval system, is forbidden without the written permission of the editorial office, Steeple Hill Books, 233 Broadway, New York, NY 10279 U.S.A.

This is a work of fiction. Names, characters, places and incidents are either the product of the author's imagination or are used fictitiously, and any resemblance to actual persons, living or dead, business establishments, events or locales is entirely coincidental.

This edition published by arrangement with Steeple Hill Books.

® and TM are trademarks of Steeple Hill Books, used under license. Trademarks indicated with ® are registered in the United States Patent and Trademark Office, the Canadian Trade Marks Office and in other countries.

www.SteepleHill.com

Printed in U.S.A.

And we know that in all things God works for the good of those who love Him, who have been called according to His purpose.

—*Romans* 8:28

To my mom and dad who encouraged me to read and write my entire life.

To my Grammy who always told me everything is possible when you put your faith in the Lord.

To my husband, Gary. Thanks for your faith in me, and for putting up with all the burned burgers on the grill and the unmatched socks in the basket. I love you.

To my children, Kara and Martin. May you realize your dreams are within your grasp when you place your faith in the Lord.

Thank you my Lord Jesus Christ for listening to my prayers all these years. Without You, my dreams would have been nothing but ashes.

Acknowledgments

Leslie Ann Sartor, I would've given up a long time ago if not for you and your incredible enthusiasm. Theresa Rizzo, you made movie nights and writing retreats an adventure I'll never forget. All the Seekers who have supported and advised me through the ups and downs of contests and rejections. The Lord knew what He was doing when he brought the 15 of us together.

Connie Rinehold, Narcy Hogan, and Janet Edgar. Each of you saw something in my writing that made you reach out and keep me on track. Thanks for stepping up and making a difference.

Extra special thanks to Melissa Endlich for scooping me off the Island and making my dreams come true.

Chapter One

"C'mon! Just a few more gates!" Jason Hunter shook his video game. Beeps and twangs filled the air.

"Jason, shaking it won't make the game go faster." Melanie Hunter flicked her gaze between the dirt road and her eight-year-old son. Along one side, rocks and pines lined the steep grade. On the other side, soft road base rimmed along a slope scorched by wildfire burn. In the middle, nothing but rough washboard dirt.

Her tire hit a bump. She clutched the steering wheel. Maybe she should have just dealt with the road construction on the interstate instead of threading around on smaller roads. With all the recent rain, the county road drove more like an all-terrain vehicle track. "Honey, sit back. I can't see."

Jason dropped the game onto his lap. "The batteries died and I was winning."

"We don't have too much farther to go. I've heard there's a ski area up here somewhere."

"It's summertime, Mom. You can't ski in June."

"No, but Twin Buttes has lots of stuff to do even if it's not snowing. We'll stop there, have lunch and poke around the town." The frown on his face said he wasn't buying into the plan. She leaned over and bumped his shoulder. "I'll bet we can get batteries there, too."

"Whatever. Couldn't you have found a job closer to home?"

Melanie sighed and straightened in her seat. *Not a job like this.* If she got the analyst position in Montrose doing research on high-altitude seeds and plants, she wouldn't be putting in the long hours at the lab like she was now. Sure, Colorado Springs was a nice city, but it was hard for her to make ends meet on her single-mom budget. Besides, Montrose offered small-town living in the Colorado Mountains. Surely she'd find something to distract Jason from video games and get him outside playing. He needed fresh air and other kids, not dark rooms and Mario Brothers' parties.

Jason dug into his backpack, pulled out a cord and aimed the plug of his video game unit at the dashboard. He missed the cigarette lighter receptacle and hit the heater knob. "Quit driving over the bumps, Mom!"

Seeing a clear stretch ahead, she leaned over and grabbed the power cord from his hand. She'd find distractions for him later; right now, she needed to concentrate on driving. The truck shimmied in the mud. She jammed the plug into the socket and carnival music came alive from the player. "Jason, sit back."

"Mom! Watch out!"

The nose of her truck headed toward the slope crest. Jerking the steering wheel, she swerved away from the embankment. Mud and gravel splattered across the windshield as the pickup shimmied across the road toward a gigantic boulder. She yanked the wheel in the other direction, fishtailing the truck.

They skidded toward another boulder at the edge of the slope, the rough and chipped face looming fast. The front corner of her truck crumpled into solid rock, stopping their uncontrolled slide. Her head hit the side window with a thud.

A shrill whistle filled the cab of the truck. She blinked. Jason sat dazed.

Sixth grade...that was as far as she'd gotten. She drew a shallow breath, glad her entire twenty-nine years hadn't flashed before her eyes.

She wrapped her arms around Jason and squeezed tight. "You all right, big guy?"

"Um hm." Wide-eyed, he stared out the cracked windshield. Seconds passed before he wiggled out of her embrace. He dumped his video game onto the floor and peered over the dashboard, his hand working his door handle with no success. "Cool. This is better than Cave Raiders any day. Look! Smoke and everything!"

Melanie lifted her fingers to massage the bump on her forehead. *Cool* wasn't exactly the word she'd use right now.

His seat belt already unsnapped, Jason scooted to the edge of the bench seat, taking in the entire mountain scene.

He plastered his nose to the passenger window. "Bet this hill makes a great sledding track in the winter." He reached across her for the door handle. "Let me out. I want to see how much truck we have left."

"The truck is fine." Melanie ruffled his sandy blond hair searching for blood. Satisfied he'd live, she smiled at the long-lost excitement in his eyes. She hoped the interview tomorrow paid off. She wanted more adventure for both of them.

She squeezed his shoulder. "It'll take more than a bump to keep us down."

Unbuckling her seat belt, she leaned into the door. Gravity worked against her. She shoved until the door groaned open. Her foot sank ankle deep into the rut. Mud oozed over the top of her boot to her toes.

Jason bumped the door wider. Losing her balance, she rolled off the seat as she wrenched around to grab the door frame. Her other foot slid beneath the truck. With all the grace of a worn-out mattress, Melanie hit the road square on her back and slid a good foot beneath the truck before her boot wedged between a couple rocks. Gravel and water soaked her arms and back. Her bottom sank into the mud, burying her legs.

"You all right?" Jason leaned out and looked around. "You're a mess."

"Thanks." She swiped her hair out of her eyes.

Jason launched over the worst of the puddle and landed on the high spot of the road. He squatted beside the rear axle and examined her like an unfamiliar specimen. "You just needed to jump out farther, Mom."

"Thanks, Jay. I'll remember that next time."

An engine rumbled in the distance. Jason bolted to the middle of the road. "I'll flag 'em down. Maybe they can pull us off the cliff."

Melanie squinted over the edge. "It's not a cliff."

"Close enough." Jason waved his arms in the direction of the noise.

"Gabe, look up ahead."

Gabe Davidson glanced up from his clipboard. His cousin pointed at a pickup truck alongside the road. From where Gabe sat, he would have said the truck wasn't going anywhere soon. "Don't recognize it."

"Can't say the truck or the kid or the blonde are from around here." Hank downshifted and slowed.

"Fishtailed right into the rock." Grooved tracks left ruts inches deep. "The boys from county won't be happy when they have to come up and fix this."

The boy waved his arms at them. Hank pulled over and cut the engine.

Gabe checked his watch. The vet closed in half an hour. He fingered the list he'd scribbled on the scrap piece of paper. If he waited until tomorrow, he'd have to take a chance the vet stocked the medication he needed, since no one at the animal clinic was answering their phone, or else double back and drive into Gunnison.

He glanced at the boy, the angle of the truck and the woman wedged partway under the running board. He ground his jaw as uncomplimentary thoughts of Nick and Zac swirled through his head. Times like this, he really wished his brothers were around to help. Propping the clipboard with his list on top of the dash, Gabe shoved at his door. "Let's go pull 'em out."

"Hey mister," the boy called, as he jumped. "I think my mom's stuck."

"Are you okay?" Hank took off toward the boy while Gabe headed for the woman. The rock, the crushed front end of the pickup and the entire back end of the vehicle sat perched at an angle. No telling what the truck would do.

"Need help?" Mud covered her from head to toe. Gabe stared into blue eyes the color of mountain columbines in full bloom and lashes as thick as the foxtails that grew around them. Blond hair played across her cheek.

"No, I've got it." The palm of her hand sank up to her wrist.

He bent over and grasped her shoulders, her muscles firm within his palms. A spear of awareness shot through him as he found a grip and began to pull. The mud packed around her like a wallow sucking her hostage. As she began to slide free, she kicked her feet against the embankment.

The road base shifted beneath his feet. His hold tightened. "Be still."

Her last kick must have hit a rock. She pushed up, relieving the tension in his pull. Momentarily. The rock worked loose beneath her foot and she sank back into place.

Gabe fought for balance as he teetered on the edge. No use. He tucked his shoulders as he rolled into the mud bog with her. His elbow trenched a rut behind her and she slammed up against his chest.

Spitting mud out of her mouth, she smeared her face with

her hand. "Oh goodness." She squirmed to the side. "You okay?"

His hat lay inverted between them, the crown crushed against her ribs. He followed the line of her muddy T-shirt sleeve to her mud-matted ponytail. Her eyes sparkled wide as he drew close. "I told you to stop moving."

"I could've gotten out by myself." Her breathless voice warmed his cheek.

He swiped his hand down his face, as much to wipe away mud as to break his stare. "I'll keep that in mind."

She shimmied up the bank using the top of his boot as a foothold. "The road is in lousy condition."

"Yeah, well." Her smooth arm pressed against his chest, making simple thought difficult. "The Gunnison County road crew won't be happy about this, either."

She stiffened beside him. "This road is a disaster."

"Not if your speed is appropriate for the road condition."

She looked at him as if he'd grown another head. "What's the speed limit for horrendous?"

Gabe shoved his palm into packed road base. Confrontational wasn't what he needed right now. Luckily, Hank crouched down beside them before Gabe said something he'd have to apologize for.

"Ma'am, are you all right? Gabe isn't the daintiest creature to have land in your lap."

"Hank, get us out." Gabe needed to move, not make small talk. He leaned over her, caught her waist and pushed her up the side of the rut.

With Hank pulling, she popped out of the ditch and stumbled a good three feet from the truck. Hank offered a hand, and Gabe scrambled out from beneath the truck. Standing beside the muddy mess of a woman, Gabe regretted his moment of anger. Her woebegone look said it all.

"Sorry about getting you dirty." Her shoulders slumped

as she reached out and swiped at his sleeve. "I appreciate the help. Our truck ran into a little problem—"

"Yeah, you should've seen it, mister." The boy ran into the middle of the group. "Mom really carved an arc in the mud!"

Color glowed from beneath the grime on her face. "Jason, shush. We just took the turn a little fast, and, well—" she shrugged in the direction of the truck "—as you can see we're—"

"Wrecked." Jason grinned with pride.

She frowned. "I was going to say, 'stuck.'"

Hank laughed and swept off his hat. "Hank Barrett, at your service, ma'am. I'm the foreman of the Circle D spread just down the road."

She took a step back and drew Jason beside her, angling her shoulder in front of him. Her protective gesture goaded Gabe even worse for his earlier irritation.

"Nice to meet you, Mr. Barrett. I'm Melanie Hunter and this is my son, Jason." She nodded toward her crumpled fender and hood. "Any capable mechanics around?"

"We can probably round one up." The top of her head barely cleared his chin as Gabe took quick stock of her for injury. Wide eyes and sun-pinkened nose didn't detract from the apprehension in her tight lips. A dripping T-shirt encased her slender frame like shrink wrap around a gasket. Long legs braced; trim arms flexed. A muddy mess, but no blood in sight. "Gabe Davidson. I own the Circle D. You're not from around here."

She gave him the once-over, her arm tightening across her son. "Just passing through. Folks are expecting us in Montrose by tomorrow."

He gripped the misshapen hat against his thigh. Hard to tell what she thought of him, and frankly, he couldn't say he was very proud of his manners. He respected her reserve, considering her situation, and he extended his hand as much in apology as welcome.

Her slim fingertips slipped into his huge palm, the layer of mud between them unable to fully insulate the warm, soft texture of her skin. Heat raced up his arm like a jolt from an electric fence. "That's a long way to call a cab. I don't suppose you have a backup plan? Someone to pick you up?"

She shook her head.

"Some guy out there needs my mom to look at their plants." Jason puffed his chest. "Mom's great with bugs, too."

Gabe released her hand and hunkered eye level with Jason, thankful for the distraction. "Bugs, huh? And what are you a specialist in, Bud?"

A cheek-splitting grin displayed teeth too big for the boy's face. "I'm great at Thrill of the Chase and Raiders of the Hidden Caverns. My games are in the truck."

Gabe grinned. A kid after his own heart. "Are you now? Any good at Wheels and Karts?"

Melanie groaned beside them.

Jason ignored his mom, his eyes growing round. "Wheels and Karts? Cool. I don't have that game. I'll show you what I've got. I need my backpack." He shot over to the stranded truck.

Melanie slopped her foot around in the mud. "Jason, I doubt you'll have time to play games with Mr. Davidson. We've got to get going, remember?"

A shadow dimmed his bright eyes as he worked the door handle. "Yes, Mom."

"Mr. Davidson—" Her gaze darted between him and Jason.

"Gabe," he corrected. He kept his eye on the boy. The ground at the edge of the road had become unstable. Tough telling what might happen.

Jason continued yanking on the jammed door handle, the entire truck rocking under the force.

Melanie turned toward Jason. The mud around her shoes acted like quicksand, keeping her glued in place. "Hey big guy, get back here before—"

The crisp creak of metal filled the air as the truck shifted with a clunk, the front bumper pointing over the edge of the embankment. Gabe swallowed the knot in his throat and sprinted toward the truck.

Chapter Two

Leaving her boots in the mud, Melanie leapt toward the truck just as Jason cried out. Gabe scooped up Jason a second before she reached his side.

Like a walrus slipping into the sea, the truck sank over the edge and slid down the side, the locked wheels creating a muddy channel down the charred slope. The pickup bounced a couple times and came to a halt on a level plane just inches from the next slope.

"Wow." Jason strained to see over the edge. Gabe held on, his arm wrapped around Jason's shoulders. Melanie threw her arms around them both, tugging at what had to be six foot plus of solid cowboy until they all stepped back. Her heart pounded like a ten-pound sledgehammer and her knees went weak. Jason squirmed.

When her nerves stilled, she released her captives and offered Gabe a weak smile. "Sorry. Thank you." She tried to smile. "I guess it's your turn to play hero for all of us today."

He didn't answer. He just stared at the truck and nodded. Flecks of mud splattered his dark brown hair, but not enough to hide the sun-kissed streaks. His tan work shirt streaked with mud clung to his broad shoulders and along the corded muscles of his back. He turned and glanced at her. The unusual shade of his eyes reminded her of her favorite root beer Popsicle, a dark shade of brown shot with spikes of gold. Only this brand of treat came complete with dense, arched brows drawn over thick black lashes. Her stomach knotted at the complete picture of male irritation he presented.

She'd overstepped her bounds. She didn't usually hug strange men. She didn't really hug men at all.

Jason twisted away and frowned at the truck. "Can I go get my games now?"

Melanie stared down the mountainside. Her truck, the only dependable thing in her life, stuck at the bottom of a mud slide. A dull ache built around the bump on her head. The games weren't going anywhere—and neither were they, for that matter.

Gabe cleared his throat. "Hank, call RJ and Manny. Ask them to come up here and haul the truck down to the parts barn. Manny can get a good look at it there."

"I'm on it." Hank headed back to their pickup.

Parts barn? That sounded way too involved for her liking. She'd already ruined the man's shirt. "We don't want to trouble you. I'll call a mechanic about the damage. Maybe the garage could send a tow?"

"We'll pull it out for you." His brows furrowed as he studied her truck. "If your husband's good with tools, it would probably be better to do a bit of home garage tinkering."

Jason hung his head and kicked at a clot of road base. "I don't have a dad."

Melanie fought her cringe. Even if Paul had stuck around, she knew breaking things was more his forte than repairing. Especially promises, dreams and hearts. Stiffening her backbone, she squeezed her son's shoulder and urged him toward a felled tree across the road. "Jason, do me a favor, okay? Go see if Mr. Davidson has a pine beetle problem."

Jason wrinkled his nose before darting across the road. She

turned back to Gabe. "Mr. Davidson, if you could just give me the telephone number of a station in town?"

He tilted his head as he looked down the slope. "I doubt the boys in town will know what to do with a vehicle they can't hook up to a diagnostic machine." He shot her a weary look. "And the name's Gabe."

"They'll be up as soon as they finish the gate." Hank shut the door behind him. "When I told Manny what we had here, he couldn't hang up the phone quick enough. He'll have your truck fixed in no time, ma'am."

Melanie faltered, the reality of her situation setting in. "Wait. I have to get to Montrose. I can't just stop here."

"You have a better plan?" Guessing he knew her answer, he turned and walked back to his pickup. "It'll be tight, but the two of you can squeeze in the backseat of the cab."

Her shoulders sagged as she grabbed her boots out of the rut and hobbled after him, the mud soaking through her socks and squishing between her toes. This wasn't happening. All because of dead video game batteries and a washed-out road, her dreams of a new beginning for her and Jason were slipping away on a mud slick of their own.

Reaching down into the truck bed, he pulled out a blanket and handed it to her. "Here."

He shrugged into a rain slicker while she wrapped the blanket over her shoulders and pulled the front ends together in her fists. Not pretty, but at least she'd protect the backseat from too much mud.

A squeal echoed from across the road. Jason had found an unscorched lodgepole pine, his shimmy already placing him halfway to the top. A few more branches up and he'd be eye to eye with a squirrel.

"Jason." She waved her arm back and forth. "Come down so we can go."

He slid down between the branches and, with a short leap, hit the ground. She snagged him as he tried to run past and pointed him toward the ranch truck. His mouth fell open. "What if someone steals my games out of Ol' Blue?"

Gabe stepped up beside him and stared at the bright yellow pickup. With a smudged knuckle, he rubbed the bottom of his jaw. "Ol' Blue?"

Melanie shifted her weight. A stone dug into her bare foot. Before she could answer, Jason brightened. "Mom bought it blue and had it painted, but the name kinda stuck."

Gabe stared at the vehicle and then, tilted his head to view the slope it had slid down. A faint crease in his cheek appeared as he nodded in understanding. "I see. Stuck."

Following his gaze, the meaning of his words hit home.

She was stuck. In the middle of nowhere. Surrounded by strangers. And no one to call for help.

She couldn't even pay for repairs on her truck beyond a flat tire.

The exhilaration she'd awakened with that morning at the thought of creating a new and better life for her and Jason now sank away in the tracks of the old yellow truck leading to the bottom of the muddy slope. A sick lump settled in her stomach.

So close. She'd been so close to holding her dream.

Lord, what do you want from me?

Gabe stared out the window of the truck as Hank drove the dirt lane to the ranch house. Fence repairs demanded attention, the cattle were nowhere near sorted, and Zac waited for reports Gabe hadn't finished. If his day unraveled any more, he'd be sitting down to dinner when the rooster crowed in the morning.

On top of that, the responsibility of the auction raced through his head. He glanced down at his watch and wiped the dirt off the dial. One-thirty. A chance he'd make it to town before Doc Hutchins left on his rounds hung by a slim thread. He shifted against the seat of the truck, pressing against the spot on his lower back where Melanie had caught him in her embrace. For a moment, the urge to wrap his arm around both of them and keep them safe had swept over him. How could a man prepare for a zinger like that?

How did he recover?

Gabe caught sight of Melanie in the rearview mirror, her eyes wide and cheeks stained with color beneath the dirt. Nerves danced in his shoulder at the memory of her soft arm pressed against him as they sat stuck in the rut beneath the truck. With his weight, he could have hurt her when his foot slipped and he'd tumbled down beside her.

And then *she'd* asked if *he* was okay.

Elbow propped against the window, Gabe slumped his jaw against his knuckles. Wildfires, reduced stock and limited pasture—he'd thought he'd pretty much run the course of God's plagues.

He'd thought wrong.

The truck turned the bend and broke out of the trees into the ranch compound. A yellow Labrador retriever barked as they pulled up in front of the house. Gabe opened his door and caught a handful of scruff as the dog barreled over him, planting muddy paws across his lap and flopping against Hank. Gabe nabbed the wagging tail before wet dog hair plastered the dashboard. "Fletcher, down."

The dog tilted his head, his tongue lolling out the side of his mouth in a pant. He pawed the wheel and a sharp blast of the horn filled the air. Gabe pointed at the ground. "Out."

Fletcher scrambled back over his lap, launched off the seat and trotted toward the open door of the ranch office.

"Does he bite?" a small voice called from the back.

Gabe looked over at the boy with blond hair and blue eyes just like his mother's. "Not unless you're dinner."

A smile broke out across the kid's face. "Cool. I like dogs. Can I go play with him?"

"You bet, if—"

Jason shot through the open door faster than a squirrel after the last nut of the season. Melanie tried to catch him, but too late. "Jason, wait."

Her brows drawn, she angled her chin toward the open door. As she puffed out a breath, the family resemblance between mother and son solidified in Gabe's mind.

Hank laughed. "That boy has more energy than a coonhound on scent."

"He's been cooped up for three hours in a truck." Melanie clutched the blanket ends together.

"He's a boy, ma'am." Hank cut the engine and climbed out of the truck.

"Every inch of him, I'm afraid." She dropped back against the seat.

Gabe unlatched the door and swung around. Melanie sat squinting into the sun, making her look more like a wistful little girl than the mom of a rambunctious boy. No woman had the right to look so feminine with mud streaked across her face and an army blanket clutched to her chin. He shoved his door wide. "Welcome to the Circle D."

Angling out of his seat, he held the door open with his knee and offered a hand. Melanie pulled the edges of the blanket tighter. Gabe tugged the slicker over his head and tossed it in the back of the truck

The kitchen door opened. "Gabe? Manny said someone had a wreck on the ridge?" His mom stepped out, cup and towel in her hand. Setting them down, she hurried across the yard to the truck. Her brows shot up as she gave him a quick once-over. "What happened to you?"

"Bad road." Mud coated his back making him feel like a moth outgrowing his cocoon. He needed a shower. His guests probably wanted one, too.

"Hmm, mighty big puddle." Grace Davidson trained her keen eyesight on the newcomers. "Anything serious?"

"Just a little dent. Nothing Manny can't fix."

Melanie snagged her foot on the edge of the blanket as she slid out of her seat. The rough wool tangled around her bare ankle, throwing her off balance. Gabe circled her waist with his arm and bent down to loose the fabric. Skin as soft as the belly of a newborn foal grazed his rough fingertips.

Melanie glared at him. She bit her lip and grabbed at the blanket edge beneath her foot. Her ear pressed against his jaw. "Meet Grace Davidson, my mother."

"Welcome to the Circle D." She tilted her head and gave Melanie a high brow. "Though by the looks of it, our welcome isn't too warm."

Fishing out from beneath the blanket, Melanie held out her hand. "Sorry to be a bother. Our truck had a little incident."

The clang of steel fence panels from the loading corrals beside the barn filled the air. Gabe twisted around to see a muscular Charolais bull pace the perimeter of the pen, his furry, white head butting the rails every few feet. Charolais stock on a whole had reasonable dispositions. Just his luck to get the exception to the rule. Ol' Milk River just hadn't been able to put his rodeo life behind him.

Gabe pushed past them and ran across the compound, every muscle in his body strung tight as a new line on an old pole. The top rail of the pen rattled and he prayed the posts around the corral held in place.

"Hank. Grab the rope." He swept his hat in the air over the bull. "Manny! Open the chute!" He yelled at the bull butting his head against the dented fence panel. If the Charolais broke loose, no telling what—or who—he'd tear up. Another slam against the panel and Gabe lost his foothold on the rail. Snagging at the top post, he held tight, bracing for Milk River to slam into him again.

Chapter Three

"Jason," Melanie yelled, as she caught her son by his shirt collar. "Stay back!"

"Mom! He's going to rip down the fence!"

As Jason struggled toward the cattle pens he obviously wasn't listening to the danger in his own words. The way the fence panels rattled, she didn't doubt the whole thing might come down. "Jason, let them handle it. Stay out of the way."

Even as she cautioned him, she and Jason followed the crowd. Melanie scooped up the edges of the blanket wrapped around her and stumbled along, clenching her jaw each time she stepped on a rock with her bare feet.

She held Jason back a good distance from the pens, not wanting him to get in the way. Gabe stood on the third rail, his hat in his hand as he waved the bull away. The animal shook his head and swung around. White hide and black eyes flashed as the massive body connected with the panel again. Melanie stood in shock, sensing the waves of anger rolling off the animal.

Another slam into the panel, and Gabe lost his foothold. Melanie tasted bile as she watched him hook his arm over the top rail and regain his hold. The bull bounced against the rails.

Gabe yelled and waved his hat much like the other cowboys positioned around the pen.

Metal clanked against metal. The bull bellowed, his sights set on the open gate into another chute. The bull bucked across the pen, snorted and trotted out. Corral panels locked together and voices rose above the clamor of the disgruntled bovine.

Gabe hopped to the ground and cradled his bruised arm. Melanie searched for further danger before approaching the injured cowboy. An uncomfortable mixture of awe and fear churned in her belly. This was not the kind of place she and Jason needed to spend time. As soon as her truck got pulled up to the road, they'd be on their way. Didn't matter if she had to drive to Montrose with a dented fender.

They needed to get out of here.

"Are you okay? That bull didn't look happy."

He stood shaking his injured arm, his chest rising and falling in a rapid beat. "Nothing worse than a cranky animal having a bad day. I can't always vouch for the dispositions of the stock my brother sends home."

This was a gift? Melanie peeked through the rails at the bull standing quietly in the back pen, swishing his tail as if nothing was wrong. "So, what does your brother have against you?"

Gabe stared at her a moment. A grin tugged at his lips. "This isn't a bull for me. It's for the auction we're having." Gabe looked over his shoulder. "All the stock you see in the pens here is up for auction."

"You're going to let some poor unsuspecting person bid on that killer?" Her mouth fell open. "That's worse."

"A bull is a bull. It's the nature of the beast." His brows drew together, sharpening his dark gaze. "No one is going to buy a *killer.* The auction discloses the history of every animal."

Her heart slowed and she regained a small measure of composure. This was none of her business. What did she know about working ranches? Nothing. And she planned to keep it that way without offending her rescuer any further.

She offered a weak smile. “Good luck with that.”

His brow raised, and in the back of her mind Melanie didn’t think he’d formed a complimentary opinion of her.

“Wow.” Jason scooted around the side panel, his mouth open and eyes wide. “Are all your cows like that?”

“That would be a bull, Bud. He’d get mighty ornery if he hears you calling him a girl. Some of the rodeo stock my brother sends me have a bit of attitude.”

Jason planted his foot on the bottom rail of the panel and stared at the empty pen with wonder. “That’s a real bucking bull?”

“He was.” Gabe bent down and picked up his muddied, battered hat, slapped it against his leg and settled it on his head. He gripped the top rail and rattled the pen with force. Jason snapped around.

“Don’t ever underestimate an animal, Bud. They’ll throw you for a loop quicker than you’ll know what hit you. Do me a favor? Don’t go near this bull or any of the livestock alone. Stick with Fletcher, okay?” He stuck out his boot and swatted dust and mud from his jeans. “If you want to see any of the animals, ask me or Hank to go with you.”

“Sure, Mr. Davidson.”

Gabe hunkered down to eye level. Melanie took a step closer, her senses on high alert. If this cowboy wanted to chew someone out for ignorance, he’d better deal with her.

“Hey, Bud.” Gabe softened his tone. “Around livestock, things can happen pretty fast, and we don’t take much time with formality here. I know your mother has taught you right, but just think, if you’d seen that bull charging me, which would get my attention faster—‘Mis-ter Da-vid-son,’” he enunciated, “or ‘Gabe!’?”

“Gabe?” Jason questioned in a small voice and turned to look at her.

She caught Gabe's earnest gaze and released her breath. She nodded at Jason. He turned back to the cowboy.

Jason cleared his throat. "Gabe."

Gabe pretended to evaluate. "One more time with feeling."

Jason took a deep breath. "Gabe!"

The cowboy grinned and patted Jason on the back. "That'll get my attention every time. Gotta keep the name short and sweet."

"Like you call me Bud?"

"That's right."

Jason thought a moment, and then peered up at him again. "What will you call my mom?"

Every drop of spit dried in her mouth. Melanie swallowed hard at the thought of anyone getting hurt, including the commanding cowboy. She dropped the edge of her blanket.

"Bud, I call your Mom 'Smart enough to stay away from danger.'"

"Enough talking." Grace approached, her arms crossed over her chest. "Let the girl get cleaned up. She's beginning to look like a mummy."

Jason giggled.

"I was just getting to that." Gabe shook his head. "Can't get everything done at once."

"Maybe not." An older man dressed in jeans and green cotton work shirt came up to stand with them. "But we gotta do the important things first." He held out his hand. "Martin Davidson. Nice to meet you." He nodded at Gabe. "Gotta keep the young'uns in line."

Color rushed up Gabe's neck at his dad's assessment, and he didn't look quite as menacing anymore. Melanie grinned. She liked Martin already. "I agree. The *young'uns* get in trouble all the time."

Gabe narrowed his eyes and then winked at her. "Dad, that *young one* by your side is Jason."

Her toes beneath the blanket curled tighter.

Martin stuck his hand out to Jason. "What do you know, young man?"

"Lots of stuff."

Grace laughed. "Oh yeah? Well how about you help Mr. Martin with that gate over there while your mom cleans up?"

"Mom?" Jason glanced up at her. "Can I?"

Her stomach churned again at the thought of Jason running around unattended. "Maybe you should stick with me, honey."

"If it makes you feel better, I'll keep a close eye on him while we go check that pasture fence." Martin nudged Jason. "You ever string wire?"

Jason's eye grew wide. "No, sir."

"Well, how can a young man leave Hawk Ridge without stringing wire?" Martin peeked over at her. "We'll be real careful."

She'd make this a very quick shower. "Listen carefully to Mr. Martin, okay, Jason?"

"Thanks, Mom." Jason fell in line with Martin, and the two of them headed to a field away from the pens.

"C'mon, darlin'. Let's get you cleaned up before you catch a cold." Grace tugged on Melanie's blanket.

Melanie looked at the sprawling log ranch house and fell in step. "I appreciate the offer, but my clothes are still in the truck."

Grace shook her head. "Not to worry. We always have extras." She threw a glance over her shoulder. "Gabriel. A little soap and water might do you good, too."

Melanie snuck a peek at the well-built cowboy who'd just battled an angry bull. He stood and squinted into the sun as if wrestling with a decision. Apparently resigned, he tipped his hat back with one finger and headed down a path into the pines.

Melanie grinned as she turned back to Grace. Not hard to tell who ran the show around the Circle D.

Hair still wet from his shower, Gabe propped one leg along the top of his desk as he read the repair receipt Manny had handed him. Replacement parts for the old truck were pricier than he thought. The cost wasn't the only problem they had on their hands.

A noisy bark in the yard announced his time of grace ended. *Father, give me words to comfort the blow of this painfully expensive situation.* Gabe sensed Melanie carried a load of pride along with her penchant for responsibility.

She swept into his office on a whirlwind of dog, laughter and sunshine. "I called and rescheduled the interview. Glad they're flexible."

Oh, she has a beautiful smile. Not that he had time to daydream about Melanie Hunter, but he had noticed a couple things about her. Especially dressed in his old flannel shirt and jeans. Even back when he could fit into that size, they'd never looked that good on him.

The familiar scent of soap and shampoo filled the air as she tucked her hair behind her ear, the sunny blond strands just sweeping her shoulders. She smelled good, looked good and felt good. Gabe stood and slapped his thigh to call Fletcher. Tongue lolling out the side of his mouth, Fletch trotted over to him and heeled.

"Glad he's trained so well." Melanie caught her breath. "He'd be a handful if he didn't listen."

"Don't let him fool you. Fletcher has his own agenda most of the time."

Her laughter faded to a smile as she looked around his office. "Nice place you have here."

Stacks of paperwork were piled around his desk and heaped onto the floor. Magazines and periodicals flowed over his filing cabinet. A cup of coffee gathered dust on the side table. Gabe winced. "Someday I'll unearth my desk."

"Never know what you'll find." She tapped a stack with her finger. "Looks like filing isn't a priority, is it?"

"You may not believe this, but I know where to find all the important stuff."

She wrinkled her nose. "You're kidding, right?"

"I think better when all my work is in front of me."

"Looks like you're shaping a trail to the barn."

Her even white teeth matched the sparkle in her eyes. His balance faltered when he realized she smiled at him. Gabe grabbed the folder from the nearest stack and indicated the chairs in front of his desk. "Here, have a seat. I have some news for you."

Melanie shot him a wary glance and stood her ground. "Good news or bad? Doesn't matter. I think I'll take my news standing up."

"I have some of both for you. The good news is that Manny can fix your truck as soon as the parts get here."

"That's great!" She hurried toward the door, her cheeks flushed with excitement. "Sorry to bother you, but maybe you can give us a lift into town where we can rent a truck for a few days?"

"I can take you anywhere you want to go. But wait, there's a bad side to this news, too."

She stopped and turned. Her round eyes narrowed and her slender frame stiffened as if awaiting a blow.

Gabe drew a breath. "Older trucks like yours are easy to putter with, very few complicated electronic parts to get in the way. The problem you have is the major component you need won't get here for at least two weeks." He handed her the page of internet research on parts and ship times.

"Two weeks?" Her voice remained steady as she scanned the page.

Gabe glanced at the remaining paperwork in his hand and winced. "There's more." He handed her the parts estimate.

She sucked in a breath and snapped her gaze up to meet his. "Is this a joke?"

His stomach pitched against tense, tired muscles. "No joke. Your truck may be simple to repair, but the parts aren't mass-produced any longer. The common parts will be interchangeable, but something as large as a radiator, well…" he trailed, praying for the right words. "Let's just say it took a bit of searching to find a used one for your make and model that inexpensive. Insurance?"

Melanie eased into the nearby chair and set her elbows on his desk. "Liability. I can cover the other guy, not myself."

His standard offer to pray with her and ask for the Father's help was on the tip of his tongue, but for some reason, he hesitated. He leaned against the edge of his desk. She'd never indicated how strong her faith was, or even if she had faith at all. Trust in the Almighty remained Gabe's answer, even if it meant holding his words at the moment. *Okay, Lord, so what do I do?*

"I've waited so long for a job like this to come up." Her voice almost a whisper as she compared the two pieces of paper. "Now, even if I get it, I won't be able to pay this *and* move." Eyelids closed, she tipped her head back. "I guess I'll cash in my vacation time and just go back to work." She sat up straight and blinked. "I have to tell Jason."

Her agony twisted his gut. "How much time did you have?"

"Three weeks. Three long, glorious weeks."

Gabe glanced at his calendar. Just enough time. "I might be able to help you."

She looked up. Any spark of light in her eyes, gone.

It was a long shot, but he'd never know until he asked. "Look around this office. I haven't a dream of catching up any time soon."

She looked around. "Looks more like a nightmare to me."

He shook his head. "Seasonal deadlines. Stock reports, financials, the like...and I have this barbecue planned for the Fourth of July."

Her brows drew close as if trying to make sense of his rambling.

"It's just a simple barbecue picnic to go along with the auction." He rushed on before she refused. "Plan for about a hundred families. You'll have help from the local ladies with food. They've been this route before—you just need to be the one in charge." He held his breath as he eyed her frozen features, worried she might explode any moment. "Don't worry about the auction. I'll take care of that."

Seconds passed before her clenched jaw relaxed. She tilted her chin and squinted up at him. "You want me to plan a party?"

Gabe leaned across the desk and slipped the two-page estimate from her fingertips. He scanned the amount again before turning the printed sheets toward her. It was worth it to him if it was worth it to her. "If you help me out with this barbecue, I'll pay for the repairs, provide a place for you to stay, and cover any costs of changing your plans."

Melanie reclaimed the sheets from him and stared at the pages. Gabe shot bullets of prayer toward heaven on behalf of her decision. She pressed her lips together and leveled a cold, clear glare in his direction. "I don't really have a choice, do I?"

Nothing could have knocked the air out of him faster than the tone of her accusation. Gabe looked out the window at a tractor idling beside the loading chute. No, he hadn't given her any choices. In his haste to solve his own problem, he'd never considered the importance of her plans. "Yes, you have a choice."

She raised a brow.

"I'll loan you a ranch truck free of charge. Use it as long as you need. Return the truck when your pickup is fixed."

He pulled out his chair, careful not to topple the pile of statements for Zac. Sinking into his seat, Gabe mentally organized his priorities for the day. He'd hoped to have an early evening tonight, obviously—

"Why would you offer the use of your truck? You don't even know me."

Suspicion, distrust, anger warred across her face. All thoughts of his personal convenience evaporated as his irritation piqued. "What do I need to know? You need transportation, don't you?"

She wrinkled her nose at him, reminding him of Jason when Fletcher wouldn't release the ball. Guess he knew where the boy got his intense concentration.

Melanie stood. Her blond hair brushed her shoulder blades as she crossed to the open doorway. Gabe caught his breath when she stopped and turned toward him, the yellow flecks in her brilliant blue eyes danced in anger.

"I'll be back." She glared a moment longer and then pushed away from the doorjamb.

Gabe blew out his breath and watched her stalk across his yard. Famous last words, but really, could he blame her?

Chapter Four

This wasn't how it was supposed to go.

Melanie propped her elbows on the fence panel and stared at the three cows in the pen. The field lab up in Montrose embodied every dream she'd ever had for her and her son. She could leave the impersonal, demanding research position she'd held for the last six years and work outdoors, on a schedule of her own. Live in a small community where maybe she and Jason could build a home.

She shielded her eyes against the rays of brilliant sunshine as they dipped in and out of darkening clouds. Late afternoon came quickly in the high country as she struggled with her decision. When she'd called to reschedule her interview, the secretary switched her to the last spot available for interviews. More than enough time to rent a car and make her appointment. And she still could, except for that little repair invoice.

An outrageous dollar amount she couldn't begin to consider shouldering.

Her meager savings allowed them a cushion for emergencies. Not a catastrophe like this. Melanie hung her head and kicked the ground.

Lord? There's a big hitch in our plans. Talking to God

was easy. She dug the toe of her sneaker into the grass patch surrounding the fence post. It was listening for the answer that got her every time.

The buzz of a four-wheeler echoed in the distance. Hank drove across a field with Jason clutched behind him. The pair rode along the fence line, Jason squealing at every bump. Melanie relaxed. Jason would love it here while she worked off her debt. She couldn't argue the fact that the great outdoors commanded his attention. Her nerves stopped their riotous zing and she blew a sigh. Funny, Gabe hadn't even asked her if she could cook.

The sweet scent of pine tinged the air as birds offered their individual tunes. Melanie closed her eyes as she tilted her face to the warm summer sun.

There were no guarantees in life. Maybe she'd get the job; maybe she wouldn't. Either way, if she left now, she'd be paying off a repair bill on an old truck for months to come.

Lord, why did you fill me with hope only to tear it away?

The four-wheeler angled around the field once more. She opened her eyes to see Hank looking like Evel Knievel and Jason sporting a smile a mile wide. Melanie shook her head.

At least she'd tasted the dream of a new job and a lighter work schedule. That taste had made her realize she never wanted to go back. Lucky her.

A door slammed in the distance and Gabe followed the walkway toward her. She tried not to look too obvious as she stared like a schoolgirl.

His button-down shirt fit his shoulders, the sleeves rolled to the elbow. Tan arms matched his suntanned face. Faded blue jeans cinched at the hip with a worn leather belt.

Tall and strong.

An incredible smile…

Melanie blinked and turned away. No need to romanticize the man, especially since she'd be working for him.

He jingled a set of keys at her. "Let's get you a truck and you can be off first thing in the morning."

He stood before her all tall and dark and cowboy, looking almost afraid…of her? She had a feeling disappointing women wasn't Gabe's strong suit. Accepting disappointment wasn't exactly high on her list either.

"I'll do the barbecue." The words tumbled out. "I mean, yes, I'll organize the barbecue for you in exchange for repairs on my truck. That is, if the offer is still open."

Gabe pushed back his hat and rubbed his forehead. "You're the answer to my prayer. We planned the auction and barbecue for the Fourth of July weekend. That's less than three weeks, and I'll help anyway I can."

"Just three weeks, right? That's all the time I have." He had to understand she couldn't give any more. "This picnic and the repairs to my truck will be done in three weeks?"

He gave a quick nod, his root-beer-colored eyes sparkling.

"And you said there were some ladies to help me out with the planning?" Melanie rushed to confirm.

Gabe tilted his head, and she received the full brunt of his excitement. His grin deepened the dimple in his cheek and added a boyish charm she could only stare at.

"From church. The ladies will point you in the right direction. As a matter of fact, we can talk to them Sunday after the service. They'll love meeting you." He indicated the path up to the ranch house. "Let's go get a key to the cabin before it rains."

Before it rains. Famous last words.

Rain blew sideways, pelting them like BBs as they stood on the porch of cabin number one. Melanie shifted beside him and clutched her duffel so her rain slicker covered most of the bags. Jason huddled up against the wall.

Gabe stuck the key into the lock, jiggled the knob and

shoved the door open. "Here we are. Sorry things might be a little dusty. We haven't had anyone live here this season."

He stepped through the threshold and stomped his boots on the mat. Melanie piled in behind him, Jason on her heels. She set her bags down on the floor beside the table and glanced around at the knotty pine cabinets lining the wall of the small galley kitchen and a window with white panes set over the sink. A peal of thunder shook the ground as rain battered the pines outside the window.

Melanie shivered beside him. "Are you sure we aren't putting you out by staying here?"

No better place on the ranch for their guests than the log cabins tucked up in the pines away from the house. Both houses. "The cabins are for the summer help. Their families visit when they can. Since the drought last couple years, we've cut back operations. We won't be needing it."

Jason dropped his bags at the door and raced through the two-bedroom cabin, poking into every nook and cranny. "Look, Mom. We each have a bed." He cannonballed onto the mattress.

A gust of wind blew rain across the threshold. Melanie stepped back and closed the door behind her. "Jason, why don't you unpack?"

"I get this room." He rolled off the bed, grabbed his pack and unzipped the top. Turning it over, he dumped the contents out on the bed.

A mountain of video game cards poured out of the bag, followed by a pair of jeans and socks. Gabe chuckled at the necessities of life. "Hey, Bud, sure you have everything?"

Jason picked up his game unit and waved it in the air. "This is all I need."

Melanie rolled her eyes. "Thanks for taking care of my truck. Sorry we disrupted your schedule."

"Not a problem." He opened the utility closet door and switched on the furnace. Five metal clicks confirmed the unit operational. Seconds later, air blew up beside him from the floor vent. "Meals are part of the deal, too."

"You're kidding, right?"

"There is nothing funny about how Grace Davidson views hospitality." He opened the linen closet and checked the towels and blankets. "Dinner is at six o'clock. Don't be late or the cook will have your hide."

"Oh no, we couldn't. You've already done so much for us."

Her blue gaze darted about the room before landing on him. She shifted her weight as if she'd had enough for one day. He couldn't blame her. His family was a bit overpowering at times. "If you're up to it, you can go in and argue. But I'll warn you, my mother drops the biggest guilt bombs you've ever seen."

Gabe backed up toward the door and reached for the knob. "That clock in the kitchen tells the right time, and the stove runs on propane. If you need anything, give a holler." Before she could respond, he made his escape, closing the door behind him.

Out on the porch, the wind continued to blow. He pulled his hat in place and stepped out from under the eave. Rain poured from the heavens. He followed the well-worn path from the cabin to the ranch house. The small stream coursing through the ruts would wick into the ground by morning.

Melanie agreeing to coordinate the barbecue was a blessing, but the added distraction of their guests threw his entire schedule off. Gabe turned at the fence corner and walked toward the office door.

Gabe had ideas and plans for the ranch operation. He had the tools and knowledge to trim time and cost; he just needed to convince his dad the changes were viable. Too often it seemed like Dad expected him to run cattle and keep tally of the stock on a wallboard in the barn much like his grandpa had.

The Fourth of July auction would make or break him. He needed to concentrate on the task at hand and make this stock sale the best of the summer. The best ever.

When he reached the deck off the office, he stomped on the worn doormat and glanced over his shoulder at the green roof of the cabin poking through the trees. On top of all the headaches screaming for attention, a new distraction now resided in a cabin out the office back door.

Lord, grant me strength.

The next morning, Jason sat in the back seat of the pickup, his arms dangling over the front seat. "I'm lost. Do you ever get lost driving into town?"

"Been driving down this road all my life." Gabe held the steering wheel with one hand as they rounded a corner. "Don't think there's anything to forget."

"I don't think I'd find my way back."

Melanie had to agree. They'd turned and twisted up and down so many little roads before hitting the main highway, she didn't have a clue how to get back. She shifted in her seat and nodded at him. "I think that's why Gabe came with us today."

After the torrential rain the night before, the sky ahead of them shone crystal blue. Melanie tensed as Gabe hit a few ruts and puddles, his truck occasionally skidding. Gabe didn't look rattled. The county roads still spooked her.

Gabe downshifted down after hitting a deeper pothole. "No sense in an instant replay of yesterday."

"Thanks." She pried her hand off the dashboard.

He chuckled. "So where do you want to stop first?"

"We need Coco Snaps and milk." Jason started the list. "Miss Grace cooks really good. I don't think Mom has to cook any meat or vegetables."

"Jason Hunter." Melanie couldn't believe her ears. "Remember your manners."

"Don't worry about it." Gabe turned down the main street of town. "My mom will be feeding him every chance she gets."

"But still." She shot Jason a warning look. "I guess we do need to stop at the grocery store."

Gabe pulled into a space down a side road. He slipped out of the truck, circled around to her side and opened the door before she had her seat belt off. Unaccustomed to the courtesy, Melanie stared at him.

"Why'd you open the door?" Jason pushed against the back door and hopped out. "Was the lock stuck?"

Gabe held the door. "A lady never opens her own door."

"Mom always opens her own door, even when she's sick."

Uncomfortable being the topic of discussion, Melanie grabbed her purse and angled out of the cab. "I'm made of sturdy stuff."

Gabe closed the door behind her and indicated the sidewalk. "Bud, a man's got certain obligations, and showing respect to a lady is the biggest one."

"I don't see why it's a big deal." Jason frowned and jammed his hands in his pockets. "It's not like she broke her arm or anything."

Gabe ruffled Jason's hair. "We have a long way to go, don't we?"

Melanie snapped to attention. Her mind whirled around their conversation even as her heart beat faster. Just because Gabe Davidson demonstrated common courtesy and a more-than-capable attitude was no reason to start fantasizing about the man. Hadn't she learned anything from past experience? Her fists tightened as she listened to Jason and Gabe discuss the finer points of good manners. She shook her head. *Get a life.*

Her world of plant and insect research offered few choices of husbandry options beyond the realm of livestock genetics. Professors, over quiet dinners and coffee, enjoyed her quick mind and attention to detail but drew the line when invited to soccer games and school conferences. The other researchers in her department viewed the world through mugs of beer and late-night parties. They hadn't a clue as to what parental responsibility entailed. And she'd never been interested in the singles scene. Not many choices left, were there?

"After you." Jason giggled as he held open the door to the grocery store.

Gabe rolled his eyes. "Yep, a long way to go."

Melanie cringed, not sure if Gabe made a habit of instilling etiquette in young boys, or if she'd just been insulted.

They ran through the store grabbing the essentials, Gabe taking them down each aisle to make sure nothing was forgotten. When they reached the cashier, Gabe inched the lid off a canister while Melanie unloaded the cart.

He handed Jason a strip of meat. "Here, try this."

Jason scrunched his nose. "What is it?"

"Elk jerky. Best you'll ever taste."

"Eww." Jason backed up.

Gabe tore off a piece with his teeth. He chewed a couple times and swallowed. "Have you ever tried it?"

Jason eyed the strip. "No."

"Do I look like I'm going to die?"

Jason giggled. "No."

"Well?" Gabe pointed the jerky expectantly toward Jason.

Melanie held her breath. Jason stared at Gabe as if he'd just offered a dose of poison, but took the snack anyway and tore off a bite. By the time all was said and done, Melanie had two bags of groceries, Gabe a dozen strips of jerky with Jason running behind him begging for another piece.

"Let's get this stuff in the truck. I need to stop by the animal clinic before we leave and Leon's Hardware for a few parts." Gabe stuffed the bags in the back of the cab. "*Some* of the fittings for your truck are easy to find."

The sun and fresh mountain air had lifted her spirits.

Melanie shaded her eyes with her hand. "Remember, three weeks to get my beloved truck as good as new."

"Promise." Gabe gave his best Boy Scout pledge.

They rounded the corner of the block. Hoses, rakes and wheelbarrows lined either side of a set of open double doors. A sandwich-board sign sat on the sidewalk and proclaimed Spring Sale—Hurry In. A wooden palette held stacks of fertilizer bags with plastic buckets displayed across the front, two rows deep.

"I love this place." Melanie listened to the delicate tinkle of wind chimes arranged from the rafters. "Very homey."

"If Leon doesn't have it, you don't need it." Gabe indicated they enter the store. "So far, he's proven his motto right."

"Gabe." A petite woman in her early twenties with curly brown hair and freckles across her nose stood behind the checkout counter and waved. "You're early. It's not Saturday yet."

"Guests staying at the ranch. Thought maybe they needed to pick up some stuff." He stepped around the counter and gave her a hug. "Shayna, I want you to meet my friends, Melanie and Jason."

When Gabe stepped back, Shayna turned around and presented a well-rounded belly. By the looks of it, probably seven months along. Out of habit, Melanie glanced at Shayna's left hand, surprised to see her ring finger bare.

"Don't think I've met you before. This your first time to Hawk Ridge?" She offered her hand. "Normally I hug everyone, but Buster here—" she ran her hand over the top of her belly "—gets in the way these days."

"I can imagine." Melanie liked the bubbly personality, especially remembering how tiring those last few months of pregnancy were. "Like the name—Buster."

She caressed her belly with love. "Only because he's ready to bust out. I'm really leaning toward Adam."

"Dad's name?"

"Oh, no!" Dimples bracketed a sweet smile. "I just like Adam."

"This is more baby talk than I need." Gabe gave Shayna another squeeze. "Bud, how about you and me go over to the parts? We've got a list we need to fill."

His gaze lingered on her as he stepped away from the counter. For a moment, she thought he'd hug her, too. Instead, he motioned for Jason to follow. "Are you going to be okay without us?"

"I think I'll survive." Melanie bit the inside of her cheek watching Jason puff up tall beside Gabe.

As they walked off to the back of the store, Shayna leaned over the counter and exhaled. "It's been a long day." She looked over her shoulder at the young man stacking a display of windshield wiper fluid in the store window. "Hey, Russ, watch the counter. I'll be back."

Russ nodded and went back to work.

"Tough working when we have a sale." Shayna stretched her back. "All I seem to do is waddle through the store."

"I remember." Melanie nodded. She swatted at a couple of tiny black insects. "Especially when all I wanted to do was sleep."

"Amen. So are you looking for anything in particular?"

Memories of her own pregnancy flooded over Melanie. Luckily she'd finished her last semester of her undergraduate degree while she was pregnant. She couldn't imagine running across campus with a baby in tow. Tough enough juggling study time in between doctor appointments, work and laundry. Her heart went out to the salesgirl. "Actually, the cabin has all I need and we're only staying a short while. Maybe a fruit bowl?"

"Right over here." Shayna turned toward the center aisle.

Melanie waved away a few more pesky gnats. "Gabe said you'd have everything we need, or we didn't need it."

"That's my dad's motto. He's pretty proud of knowing

what the town needs." Shayna stopped in front of a display of ceramic bowls. "I'll let you in on a secret. If he doesn't have it, he'll order it and then pretend he found it in the warehouse. It's a game and everyone knows, so it really isn't a secret at all."

"Thanks for the insider tip." Melanie slapped a gnat on her arm. "Does the store stock plants? I think you're overwatering."

Shayna nodded and pointed an aisle over. "We just received a shipment. Noticed they came in kind of buggy. Don't know what to do about it other than pray they get bought soon."

"Let me see." Melanie approached the display of leafy houseplants stacked in the middle of birdbaths, ceramic pots and a water fountain. "The fungus gnats are breeding because of the moisture. Here." She grabbed a package off the shelf. "Put these yellow sticky tapes around the pots for a couple of days. You should see a big difference." She dug her finger into the soil. "If you stick raw potato slices in the pot, it'll help catch them, too."

"That's great." Shayna snagged the package of tapes and tore it open. "What did you say you're doing here?"

"Normally I work with stuff like this. But for the next three weeks—" she held her arms open to embrace the entire concept "—I'm planning the Fourth of July barbecue at the Davidsons'."

Shayna laughed so hard, Melanie thought she might go into labor right then. "Don't understand how he roped you into it and don't think I want to know. So, Gabe is shirking his responsibilities. Gabe!" She stood on tiptoes and yelled for him again. "Melanie seems like a nice person. Why saddle her with the picnic?"

Gabe and Jason came round the corner. He lifted a brow and winked at Melanie. She couldn't help it and winked back.

"I'm doing my part for the event, honest. It's just that Bud and I have this truck to fix, and fence to check, and water to fill, and—"

"Yeah, yeah, I know all about the important stuff." Shayna waved him away. "Melanie, don't you worry about the picnic. The ladies at church know how to do it all. I'll be helping, too." She grinned and nodded in his direction. "Gabe's too chicken to work with us on the committee."

The red infusing his face gave truth to the accusation. "Do tell." Melanie played along. "Sweet little church ladies?"

He tipped his hat back, eyes opened wide. "Worse than a pack of starved kittens around a bowl of milk." He shook his finger at her and grinned. "Don't you let them weasel out of making the best steaks a man's ever tasted. I'm counting on you to handle this assignment with kid gloves."

Shayna elbowed her in the ribs. "Stick with me. Gabe will end up getting the glory, but we'll know who did all the work."

He offered Melanie a lazy smile. "I always give credit where credit is due. I think this year we'll have one of the best parties ever. And I'll make sure everyone knows who was in charge." He indicated the spare parts in his hands. "Hopefully terms equitable for both parties."

Chapter Five

That evening, Melanie sat at the dinner table in the ranch-house kitchen, now cleared of dishes. Homemade chicken and dumplings with all the fixings and the best berry pie with vanilla ice cream she'd ever tasted. She resisted patting her tummy. Life just didn't get any better.

In the next room, Jason yelped, "No fair, Gabe! I didn't know that boulder was going to roll onto the track."

"Well, Bud. You better be prepared for the unexpected next time." A hardy laugh echoed into the kitchen. "Had enough?"

"Uh-uh. I'm ready for you this time."

"All right. One…two…three…" A buzzer sounded as the go-kart video game took off again.

Well, life could be a little better. Grace stood at the kitchen counter watering her plants. Martin had joined the boys in the living room. Melanie set her cup down.

"Grace, are you sure I can't help you with anything?"

"Oh my, no." She shook her watering can. "Gotta give my little buddies a drink before they go to sleep."

"Plants don't stand a chance at my home. After working with them all day, I forget to tend them at night. Jason knows chocolate is the way to his mom's heart."

"My boys used to drag home every weed the good Lord planted on the mountainside. Said they were pretty flowers, and so many of them, no one would miss 'em. I praised them for their thoughtfulness and prayed none of the seeds scattered on the way home."

"You have two other sons, right?"

"I do." Grace nodded. "Nicholas and Isaac. All three of the boys have grown into men I'm proud of."

The sounds of the video game echoed in the background, Gabe's full-bodied laughter causing her heart to trip. Melanie took a sip from her cup. If the other two brothers were anything like Gabe, the women of Hawk Ridge needed to watch out. "Where are they?"

"Zac's in Denver. He went to college there and decided to stay."

Grace returned to the sink and refilled her watering can. "Nick got a burr in his drawers one day. Hawk Ridge wasn't where he wanted to be. Left the house he built up on the ridge and everything. He'd rodeoed all through school and thought he'd take off and see the country on the backside of a bull. He's the one sending the cattle for the auction."

"Sounds like exciting lives." She scooted to the edge of her seat. "I'll bet you miss them."

"Well, it's good for them to find out what they really want. Gabe never really wanted to go anywhere. He went to school in Gunnison for four years and then came home to do exactly what he'd done his whole life."

"Awww, c'mon, Gabe." Jason whined from the other room. "That water came out of nowhere."

"Bud, you had to know it was coming." Buttons clicked. "You're driving right next to a river."

"No fair…"

"You're a lap behind. Stop bellyachin' and get to movin'."

A tiny bell tinkled each time the cars made a lap. Melanie watched the entire game—and cringed.

"And what about you, Melanie? You and Jason getting by?"

Melanie took a sip of her coffee and held the cup to her lips. A loaded question if she'd ever heard one. What kind of answer was Grace looking for? She took another sip and lowered her cup. "We take each day as it comes."

"Does Jason get to see much of his dad?"

Okay, Grace. Just cut to the chase. "He never met his dad." Melanie lowered her eyes, still unable to completely justify the past. She blew a quick sigh. How things could have been different. "He's been gone a long time."

Grace dropped the water can on the counter and wiped her hands on the dish towel. "Oh, honey. I'm sorry."

"It's okay, Grace. It's been a long time." Melanie frowned as the older lady sat down beside her, grabbed her fingers and squeezed. She wanted to pull away, but Grace kept hold. "We're fine."

"Happened to my oldest boy, Nick. They hadn't been married but a couple years when his wife died. He hasn't been right since." She squeezed tighter and shook her head. "Death can do awful things to those left behind."

Paul? Dead? Melanie opened her mouth to correct the misunderstanding and then pressed her lips together. Paul might as well be dead to them. And she didn't know Grace or the family well enough to explain the entire story.

Jason didn't even know the whole truth.

"I'm sorry for Nick's loss, Grace." She searched the kitchen for words. "Time heals all hurts."

Grace nodded. She patted Melanie's hand before sliding her palm back and reaching for a napkin to blow her nose. "Time and prayer. God knows what He's doing, even if we don't understand."

Wasn't that the truth? She'd spent sleepless nights trying to come up with answers that just didn't seem to exist.

"Do your parents help you?"

Melanie automatically cringed at the question.

Seconds later, Grace groaned. "Oh no. Losing your husband and your parents so young in life, poor thing." Grace patted her hand. "Accident or illness?"

"Neither. My folks are fine. I just haven't seen them in a while."

Grace stared at her, searching for what Melanie couldn't begin to know. Even though she hadn't known Grace long, Melanie liked her and didn't want to disappoint her, as she had her parents.

A slow nod made the gray streaks in her dark hair sparkle. "Life's too short for that, honey." Grace softened her tone. "Parents try as hard as they can to do the right thing. We're only human, living by the grace of God. All the prayer in the world won't give us the right answers for the difficult questions in life. But the good Lord knows we try."

Appalled she might have insulted Grace, Melanie scrambled. "Of course you do. Raising children is the most difficult task in the world." She pointed toward the doorway leading to the living room. "Gabe's a fine man. A gentleman to be proud of."

"All three of my boys are fine men. But that doesn't mean mistakes weren't made along the way." Grace took a deep breath. "Someday our family will be restored. Melanie, don't let the chance pass you by."

"Trust me on this one, Grace. They won't understand."

"If you trust the Lord with your life, He'll make the right choices for your life. But if you don't trust the Lord, then you'll never find out what He had in mind for you."

Easy for her to say. If the shoe had been on the other foot and Melanie hadn't wanted her child, maybe she could beg forgiveness. But how could she explain that her parents didn't accept Jason? Even after all the years, the words still tasted acid on her tongue. "It's hard to make everyone happy. Especially with difficult choices."

Grace relaxed her shoulders and refilled both their

mugs. "So tell me about this job. Do you have friends in Montrose?"

How did she explain the situation to Grace when Melanie barely understood the reasoning herself? "No, I don't know anyone there. I've never even been to Montrose."

Grace sipped her coffee, looking at her with questions in her eyes.

"I want a new start." She pushed strands of hair from her face and took a deep breath, encouraged by Grace's patient silence. "I've done nothing but research projects in an office no bigger than a bathroom for six years. Not exciting, but stable. Now, a gigantic corporation bought the company where I work. Reorganization. Cutbacks. My job is safe, but the parameters will change. Same money. More work. Less time with Jason."

She traced a pattern on her mug. "When this opportunity came up, I didn't give it a second thought. I called for an interview, packed up the truck and away we went. I've never done anything like this before."

"Is that what you want?" Grace asked in an even voice. "Adventure?"

"Adventure?" It sounded frivolous when Grace said it. "I don't need adventure. I need a solid, stable home for my son. I can't do that when I'm working sixty hours a week." Melanie stood and wandered to the sink and stared at the reverse reflection of the kitchen in the darkened window. "Jason is my world, Grace. I want to do all I can for him."

"The mark of a true mother. It's not easy, is it? You try to do everything you can to keep your children safe, but you can't do it all. Only God is perfect. We have to remember that."

Melanie released a quiet sigh. "I learned that a long time ago."

She needed to change the subject before Grace unearthed more of Melanie's failures.

Bells and sirens rang in the other room, signaling the

start of another game. She nodded toward the living room. "I so wanted to get Jason away from video games. And what happens? We end up meeting the video game king himself." Melanie blew another sigh. "This is all he does at home. He's an addict."

Grace sat silent a moment, the game ringing to announce the end of the race. "You know the more you push, the harder he'll buck, right?"

"He's only eight years old. I need to guide him in another direction before it's too late."

All emotion aside, Grace pinned Melanie with a look. "That's all well and good, but he'll always come back to the things you don't approve of and he'll probably not even know he's doing it." Grace drew a breath. "Even at eight years old, Jason thinks he knows what he wants. And he wants you to want it, too. The more you disapprove, chances are the more he'll resist, and then one day he won't be there to listen to you. Take it from me, I've been through it all."

Not exactly what she wanted to hear. "What do I do? There's more to life than video games."

"Woohoo! I beat you, Gabe! Did you see? I dodged that rock slide like a pro!"

"You sure did, Champ. Good job."

"Watch out. I've got it now!"

A low rumble of laughter filtered from the room as the buzzer rang signaling a new track. Melanie sank back into her chair. "I'm sunk."

Grace took a sip of coffee. "Have you ever told him how good he is at his video games? You know, praise him?"

She stiffened. "You've got to be kidding? Encourage him?"

"No, let him know you're proud of his accomplishments." Grace studied the mug in her hand. "All he wants is your approval. Mark my words, show him you see how good he can be at video games, and he'll want to show you how good he can be at other things. Kids want attention, good or bad. Trust me. I've raised three very headstrong boys. Praise and prayers to the Lord for patience. No better tonic around."

Squeals of joy blared in from the other room. Melanie rubbed her forehead, the inkling of a headache just above her eye.

She glanced at the clock, searching for a polite means of escape. She'd had enough soul-searching for one night. "Sorry I took up so much time this evening with my problems. The dinner and company were wonderful."

Grace waved her off. "I don't often get to share my words of wisdom with new folks who haven't heard them before."

Melanie walked into the other room where Gabe played like a pro, cool and calm, while Jason rolled all over the floor in a pattern to match the track his kart raced. Jason maneuvered his car around a sharp curve and headed down the finish line.

"I won again!"

"You're not half bad once you stop whinin'." Gabe set his controller down on the coffee table.

"Okay, kid, it's time to go," Melanie said as she swallowed her disdain for the video games.

"Aww, Mom."

Grace nudged her in the ribs.

Melanie wrinkled her nose. "You race like a pro, Jay. I've never seen you play so well."

Jason stopped in midwhine. "You watched?"

"The way you came around the turn just now and drove down the straightaway? Terrific."

Jason stared openmouthed at her. "Thanks, Mom."

"You're welcome." She caught Gabe grinning at her and felt heat warm her cheeks. Her next words stuck in her throat. "Maybe if Gabe isn't too busy, you can come by and play again before we leave."

Jason frowned and looked down at his controller. Music

played behind him, waiting for the players to pick their track. He handed Gabe the unit. "Thanks, Gabe. Maybe we can do this again, sometime?"

"Sure. Just make certain—"

"I know—" Jason lowered his voice "—chores are done first."

Gabe rumpled Jason's hair then tickled his belly. "Smarty pants."

Squeals rang as Gabe and Jason wrestled on the floor. Melanie smiled inside. Maybe she'd stumbled onto something good after all.

Gabe stopped and caught his breath. He grabbed the arm of the couch, pushed up from the floor and stretched his muscles.

Jason wrapped the cord around the controller and set it on the television. "But it's Saturday night. Mom says I can stay up later on Saturday night."

"Church time comes mighty early when you go to bed late. Better not chance it." He snagged his hat from the peg by the kitchen door and settled it on his head. Morning definitely came early. Especially when he had a couple more hours of work ahead of him. "C'mon, I'll walk you to your cabin so the wild chipmunks don't get you."

"Mom?" Jason darted past. "Are we going to church in the morning?"

"Looks like it, big guy. I have some important people to meet if we're going to get a barbecue planned." She stood by the door, her hand on the jamb. "Right, Gabe?"

"I'm sure the ladies of Faith Community will be singing their hearts out tomorrow morning." He nodded to his folks, giving his mom a quick hug. "Mom, Dad. I'll see you in the morning."

"You done for the night, Gabe?" Martin ambled over to the door.

"Just need to button up a few things."

"Not too late, son." Grace kissed him on the cheek. "Don't want to poke you awake in the pew during Pastor Dave's sermon."

Gabe ushered Melanie and Jason out and closed the door behind him. He'd had fun tonight. Jason turned out a worthy opponent. Ha, the kid even beat him a couple of rounds. Nice having human competition instead of playing the machine all the time. "How's the cabin working out for you, Melanie?"

She stepped around a rut in the lot before looking up at him. "It's nice and cozy. I know it's only been a couple days, but waking up and having coffee out on the porch is fast becoming my favorite pastime."

"I hear things crawling around in the trees all night long." Jason ran up and squeezed between them. "Are there any bears up here?"

"Always that chance, but I've never seen one." He ruffled Jason's hair. "Had a couple mountain lions a few years back. And raccoons. No bears."

Jason's eyes grew wide and his mouth fell open. "Mountain lions? Cool. Maybe we'll see one. Maybe I'll get a picture of one. Maybe we can catch one."

"Whoa, Jason." Melanie stuck out her hand. "How about we plan a picnic without the added guests? I think feeding two-legged creatures will be test enough for me this first time."

"Gabe?" Jason obviously turned from the answer he didn't want to hear. "What do ya think? Can we go looking for mountain lions?"

"Bud, always be careful what you ask for. You never know when the good Lord is going to call your bluff." He was sorry he'd said something. Mountain lions needed to stay well away from people. "I'll bet there's something a bit more tame for you to do."

"And you never know what we're going to find in Montrose,

right?" Melanie shoved her fingers into the front pockets of her jeans. "Remember, we'll still be in the mountains."

"Maybe I'll find a mountain lion up there." Jason peered past Gabe and searched through the trees. "Hey, if we can't go lion hunting, can we go four-wheeling, or play Karts again?"

The familiar pressure began to build across the back of his neck. There wasn't enough time in the day for Gabe to finish all his usual chores, let alone entertain an enthusiastic boy. "We'll see what kind of time we can come up with, okay?"

"How about catching raccoons? I've never seen a real one. You know they hunt at night." Jason began to recite nocturnal carnivore facts like an encyclopedia. "If you have to work all day, we can go at night, right, Gabe?"

Melanie reeled her excited son in by the shirttail until he bumped into her. "Jason, we're here to get a job done and we've only got a couple weeks to do it. Gabe isn't on vacation like we are. We have to let him do his work." She shot him a conspiratorial grin. "Let's not make him want to get rid of us before the truck is fixed."

Gabe grinned back, thankful for the diversion. This just wasn't a good time to entertain guests. "Seems like the work never stops. Always something to do."

"Great! I can't wait to see what we're gonna do tomorrow. This is going to be great."

Gabe rolled his eyes. We? How had one nighttime video game become an instant daytime *we?* They reached the porch of the cabin, and Gabe held open the screen as Melanie opened the door.

"Thanks for the escort. It's so dark up here with only the moon and stars for light." Melanie tipped her head back and searched the sky, the tips of her hair reaching midway down her back. "The stars look like ice chips."

Gabe followed her gaze. The inky night sky hosted tiny flecks of light, like a blanket of sparkles across the sky. "It clears up after a rain. The clouds all disappear. Makes you wonder where they came from in the first place."

"I could stand here forever."

Gabe peeked at her upturned face, her cheeks smooth and the corners of her mouth turned up. She squinted into the night as if trying to see into eternity. When was the last time he looked up into the night sky with wonder?

Enough wasting time. He had invoices to review, and they weren't getting done this way. "Well, see you in the morning."

Melanie gave him a shy smile as she turned toward the door. "Don't work too hard. Good night."

"Gabe." Jason poked his head out the door. "Get everything done tonight so we can do stuff tomorrow."

He turned on his heel and stepped down the path before Jason came up with more ideas. "Good night and sleep tight."

The door of the cabin closed behind him and the dead bolt slid into place. As he made his way down to the office, he tipped his head back and studied the night sky.

He didn't do *we*. He hadn't done *we* in years. Not since Cheryl Slaughter had dumped him, accusing him of being married to his work and informing him she had no intentions of being the other woman.

Truth was, he couldn't blame her. Who wanted to date a guy short on time and long on tasks? Ranching came first. He had to weigh his choices, pick his battles. Time didn't stretch to accommodate his schedule.

How in the world was he going to fit *we* into his life now?

Chapter Six

It's a church service, not an execution.

Sunday morning had arrived mighty fast. Melanie brushed her hair in front of the mirror, her faint cowlick making an appearance today of all days.

Nine years of bitter reality swirled through her mind, remembering the gossip and lies from friends in her singles group. The betrayal. The loneliness.

"C'mon, Mom! We don't want Gabe to leave without us."

"Just a second, honey." She was just attending a church service. Maybe two or three, max. She wasn't getting involved. They wouldn't know anything about her. They'd have nothing to judge. She studied her reflection in the bathroom mirror, careful to keep her voice steady. "I'll be right out."

"You look great." Jason poked his head in the door. "I never see anyone going to church in jeans. How come we can?"

"Because that's all the clothing we brought. Besides, the Lord doesn't care what you look like. The important thing is that you worship."

Jason frowned into the mirror. "How come we've never gone to church before?"

If she explained all her issues with the social aspect of

church membership now, they'd be in the bathroom all day. "Let's see what you think of it, okay?"

She followed Jason out the door and down the path. He scrambled into the backseat of a late-model SUV, his freshly scrubbed face grinning out the window. "Look at this car, Mom. It has a DVD player in the backseat and everything."

Melanie shook her head. Ah, the important things in life. "We're ready. Sorry you had to wait."

"You're right on time." Gabe stepped around the back and opened the door for her. Dressed in crisp jeans and a rust-patterned shirt, the look gave a formal touch to his rugged appearance.

His wet hair curled naturally behind his ears and at the collar, making her want to tug at her misbehaving bangs. Why couldn't her makeup, clothing and hair cooperate when she needed to look halfway decent? This outing was difficult enough without Gabe looking like a prince.

"After you." He indicated the open door.

Martin and Grace sat up front. Melanie slid in next to Jason, Gabe next to her. The ride to church held small talk centered around the crop progress of various fields on either side of the road. Melanie sat ramrod straight to keep from leaning against Gabe.

By the time they reached the church, it was almost nine o'clock. Finding a place at the far end, they crossed the parking lot with the other stragglers and stepped inside as the organ started to play.

The spaciousness of the sanctuary surprised her, considering the small, plain exterior of the church. Floor-to-ceiling plate-glass windows behind the pulpit made the room seem to stretch into forever. A gentle slope of green grasses dotted with yellow and blue wildflowers offered a gorgeous backdrop.

The crew slid into a front pew; Melanie followed Gabe with Jason between them. Grace offered her a hymnal. The smooth cover of the book slid into her hand, the texture of the pages as familiar as the music that filled the air. She fanned through the middle of the book, inhaling a timeless scent long forgotten.

The music stopped and the pastor gave his greeting. Unexpected calm settled over her. She didn't expect God to forgive her for staying away so long, but then, she wasn't ready to come running back into the fold, either. She looked at Jason sitting with his hands folded on his knee.

Just like his newly adopted hero.

Tall and strong, Gabe wore self-confidence as if the fit were tailor-made. He certainly wasn't afraid of her son, like all her other dates.

Dates? Whoa. No, she meant acquaintances. She didn't do dates.

Paul Margolis had been more than an acquaintance, and look where that had gotten her.

The dark memories shadowed her mind. She pushed them back. She was older and wiser now. Churches were filled with sinners. Some looked to repent, others to pray. Others simply wanted to belong.

"'...come to me all you who are weary and I will give you rest.'" The pastor offered a kind smile to his congregation. "The Lord offers you His yoke. Don't be afraid to try it on. It's the best fit in the world. Amen."

She blinked as the gentle man stepped out from behind the pulpit and the music started. Take the yoke? Hadn't she been doing that? Caring for Jason. Alone.

The service concluded, and folks started gathering their belongings.

"Follow me. I know where they keep the good cookies." Gabe winked at her as he guided Jason through the crowd. They threaded down a hallway packed with people. Gabe smiled and greeted everyone. They rounded a corner where a table sat with plates of cookies and cups of juice.

"Wow, those look good." Jason stepped closer to Gabe. "Can I have one?"

"Better grab two—the crowd will be here in no time." He leaned close to her, a hint of peppermint teasing her as he grinned. "Nick, Zac and I learned to grab cookies first, then go back and talk."

"Gabe, I thought I saw you had guests." A willowy strawberry blonde held out her hand. "I'm Jennifer O'Reilly."

Arched brows and sable lashes framed the most gorgeous green eyes that twinkled when she laughed. Melanie smiled back. "Melanie Hunter, and this is my son, Jason."

Jason waved from the cookie tray, his lips edged with chocolate chip crumbs. Jennifer waved back. "Nice to meet you. Are you here for a visit?"

"Melanie and Jason are staying at the Circle D long enough to pull together the Fourth of July barbecue." Gabe stepped back to the table and snagged a couple of cookies, offering one to Jennifer and one to Melanie.

Her jaw dropped open. "How in the world did he palm that off on you? He's been trying to get someone to take over for him since his dad insisted it was part and parcel of the auction. Oh, Melanie. We've got to talk."

Her animated words drew Melanie, yet brutal memories cautioned her. She longed to just accept people at face value. Longed to have others accept her for the same.

A tinge of red spread across Gabe's cheek. He turned toward the boys who had collected around the cookie table with Jason. "Hey Toby, Ben. This is my friend Jason. How about if you guys show him around?"

"Melanie, glad you made it to the service." Shayna squeezed through the throng of people. "That sticky paper worked wonders on the plants. Only a couple of pesky gnats left in the whole place."

"Glad I could help."

"How are you feeling, Squirt?" Jennifer came up and hugged Shayna. "Only a month or so left, right?"

"Longest six weeks of my life." Shayna hugged, then pushed away, her hands working to fan herself. She offered a halfhearted smile. "Only June and I'm so hot. Glad Dad has the fans going. Won't turn on the air-conditioning. Thinks it'll hurt Buster if I get chilled."

Melanie liked the ladies despite the warning voice in her head. Jennifer and Shayna didn't treat her like a stranger. They chatted with her like she'd been part of their circle forever. "How about at home? Does your husband feel the same way?"

Shayna snickered as Jennifer rolled her eyes. "Husband? If that worthless bum dares show his face in town ever again, he'll have to deal with us all."

Melanie froze in confusion. "But..."

Jennifer touched her shoulder with in-the-know fingertips. "High school sweetheart ran for the hills as soon as Squirt here started feeling sick."

"When I told him I was pregnant," Shayna cut in, "he dumped me faster than a load of manure. Had the whole town pestering him to do the honorable thing until he couldn't take it anymore and moved to California to live with his dad. A couple of months later, his mom left to live with her mother. The whole family ran out on me."

"Their loss." Jennifer shook her head, a frown forming across her brow. "Not a problem, though. Hawk Ridge is waiting to spoil little Adam rotten."

Her stomach soured as Melanie digested the circumstances. Shayna. Pregnant. Alone. Melanie looked around at the smiling faces surrounding her and sensed the protective shell the congregation had wrapped around their little wronged lamb.

Melanie's life had run the same course, yet her friends and family had dropped her like a hot potato. She'd been shunned by her peers and continued to shoulder the pain and guilt of her parents' shame.

Here in Hawk Ridge, the community stood by anxiously for the arrival of their bundle of joy. Back in Melanie's day, everyone she'd turned to had only wished her situation gone.

As simple as black and white.

"So, are you ready to brave the ladies' planning committee tomorrow?" Jennifer nudged her. "Are you all right?"

Melanie needed space and quiet to deal with all the old feelings that were rising to the surface. She thought she had everything under control. She thought they were getting along fine.

Just her and Jason.

"Tomorrow? Sure, tomorrow's fine. The sooner I get started the better off I'll be." Melanie looked around the crowd. "I haven't seen Jason in a bit. I better go find him. Excuse me?"

"See you then." Shayna waved.

Names and faces mulled together as she wove toward the door. Outside, Gabe's strong voice and ready smile spread across the crowd like spun sugar. She relaxed. She had just needed air.

"I see you've met the ladies." Grace Davidson hooked her elbow and indicated the edge of the parking lot. "If I don't get you away from them, you won't have an ear left for the rest of your visit."

"A welcoming bunch. Hard to find a group in Colorado Springs as friendly as this."

"Uh-huh. In a few days, we'll discuss what you really think of them." Grace grinned in conspiracy. "Martin said his shoulder hurt, so we're just biding our time over here under the tree. Come join us."

They walked across the parking lot toward the shade. Martin sat on a rough-hewn bench, a thin layer of perspiration on his forehead despite the slight breeze in the air.

"Are you comfortable?" Melanie gave him a quick once over. "I could call Jason—"

"Don't pay my aches and pains no mind." Martin rolled his shoulder and nodded to indicate the crowd. "Yep, the ladies are all ready to help you, I see. To watch Gabe milling about now, you'd never suspect he'd avoided the good ladies of Hawk Ridge for the last few weeks. Hates crowds, he does. Now that he's passed the baton for the picnic, he can relax and jaw around."

She shrugged. "He seems very good at running the ranch. Sounds like he knows what he wants."

"Gabe still has lots to learn before he calls himself boss. He'll get there in time." Martin ran his fingers over his mouth and down his jaw. "Once he settles down and can focus on ranching, I 'spect the Circle D will do just fine."

"Good for him. Good for you." She noticed Jennifer join the crowd. Jennifer laughed at some comment, clutching Gabe's sleeve with one hand, covering her mouth with the other.

For a moment, Melanie flashed back to a time when she'd laughed at Paul's comments and snuggled closer when he wrapped his arm around her. The memory poured icy thoughts down her back. She hadn't thought about Paul so much in years. Why now? She didn't want to think so hard today. "Do you see Jason around?"

"He ran around behind the church with the Wheeler boys. They're probably showing him the ropes."

"Hmm, I better learn some roping while I'm here, too."

Excusing herself, she took off and rounded the corner of the church. Squeals rang high as she saw Jason in a swing being pushed by one of the boys. The ropes of the swing suspended from a steel pipe secured between two pine trees right at the edge of a cliff. With each push, Jason swung higher and higher out over the drop-off that fell forever.

Her stomach sank as she quickened her step. She hadn't

been paying attention. In a strange place, who knew what could happen? If Jason got hurt, she'd never forgive herself.

He was all she had.

Gabe excused himself as he watched Melanie head to the back of the church. Though the building sat on a solid rock foundation, it perched on the edge of a ridge. He didn't want her to misstep and injure herself.

Just as he turned the corner, he heard her gasp. Between the pair of ramrod-straight pines, Jason swung way out wide. Gabe took one look at the terror written on Melanie's face and rushed past her, flagging down the boys. "There's a lot of power in that swing, boys. How about if we go easy on the newcomer?"

Ben grinned as he bumped the seat of the swing, sending it straight into Toby. Toby caught the rope and Jason got dumped from the plank seat to the ground. "We asked Jason if he'd ever swung over the world before. He said no. So we wanted to show him what it was like to fly."

Jason stood up and wiped the palms of his hands on his jeans. "Way cool. Mom, wanna try?"

Gabe gathered the boys and urged them back to the church. "I think your mom might try it another time. Bud, could you please find my folks? It's probably time to go."

"Jason," she rasped. "You could have—"

"—touched the branch overhead with your toes." He blocked Melanie from the boys as he approached her. "Come here, let me show you."

The boys took off running.

"Wait, Jason."

"They weren't in any danger. Do you think the church would keep the swing up if we thought anyone would get hurt?"

Melanie jerked away, not bothering to look. "Don't tell me not to worry about my son. I'm the only one who does.

I thought he was going to fall off and tumble down to who-knows-where."

"You can trust—"

"Trust?" She shot him an incredulous look. "I haven't known you long enough to develop that kind of confidence. All I saw was my son swinging on a rope and board way over the edge of a cliff." Tears brightened her eyes.

"Melanie, I wouldn't have let anything happen to him."

"I'll determine what's safe and what's not." She forced the words through tightened lips. Wiping her cheek on her shoulder sleeve, she hardened her glare. "Just leave us alone."

She turned and stalked back toward the church, her steps jarred as she stomped on stones.

Lord forgive me, I wasn't thinking. He'd treated Jason as he would've any of the town kids and overstepped his bounds. Now he desperately prayed for a way to fix it.

Chapter Seven

Lower than a snake's belly in a rut, her grandpa used to say.

Melanie paced back and forth across the back patio of the cabin. How could she explode like that? Sure, Gabe had no right to determine what was safe for Jason, but he was after all the man holding the purse strings. Where would she be right now if he nixed the deal and just sent them off the ranch? How was she going to pay for the truck repairs?

Stupid, stupid, stupid.

"Mom, what are you doing?" Jason popped his head through the door. "Let's go for a hike. There are lots of places to explore around here."

"Be with you in a second, honey."

Jason disappeared. She hung her head and studied the pine needles scattered beneath her bare feet on the back porch. She would have grounded Jason for a week if he'd behaved as poorly as she had. A door slammed at the other end of the cabin as she reached for the door handle. An afternoon hiking with Jason sounded like an excellent idea.

"Jason?" The air remained cool inside despite the warm, summer temperatures. Flies buzzed against the screen door, and a breeze carried the scent of fresh outdoors throughout the rooms. Under normal circumstances, Melanie would have loved the rustic, homey feel of the cabin. Instead, she couldn't wait to put on her hiking boots and get as far away from her thoughts of Gabe Davidson as she could.

Tying the laces of her boots, Melanie heard Jason squeal outside the door. A familiar male voice filtered through the door. A knot formed in her stomach. She had a feeling the walk they'd planned just ran into a hitch.

Jason bolted into the cabin as the screen door slammed behind him. "Mom! We're going horseback riding!"

She continued to work her laces. "I thought we were going for a hike."

"Gabe's taking us!" Jason sprinted back out the screen door with a whoop, earning another slam in the process.

"Gabe is not taking us anywhere," she muttered to herself, as she finished tying her other bootlace, grabbed a jacket and followed out the door.

Not a soul in sight, Melanie trekked down to the ranch house. Gabe and Hank stood by the corral fence. She marched down to the group, her lips pressed together. Gabe took off his hat.

"I don't believe my work week has started yet." Melanie tried not to sound harpish. "Jason and I had plans."

"I think the young man here got his signals mixed up," Gabe explained. "We came up to invite you for a ride. I told him it had to be okay with Mom, or maybe we could do it another time."

Three hopeful faces stared at her. She wanted to sink into the dirt for all the rash assumptions she'd been making lately. "A trail ride?" *Grace…tact…humor…* "Sounds like fun."

The fact that sincerity didn't match her words fell on deaf ears. Jason whooped like a convict released on parole. He ran up to Gabe, grabbed his hand and started tugging him toward the gate. "Can I ride a black horse? They're the coolest…"

Saddled horses stood patiently in the warm summer sun, their tails swatting flies in rhythm to each other. Grace and Martin stood inside the pen adjusting tack on a pair of horses.

"What took you so long?" Martin tightened the cinch on a handsome bay. "Sun's going to set before we even get going."

"Which one is mine?" Jason hiked up a rail on the fence. A black-and-white paint stuck out his nose to nudge him on the shoulder. He laughed and held his palm out for the horse to smell. "Hey, want to go for a ride?"

"That's Nipper. He's a good horse for you to get your riding legs." Gabe ducked into the corral, grabbed the reins and led the horse out. "Bud, why don't you hold the reins and talk to Nipper for a second, just let him get used to you and your voice."

Gabe explained the basics of riding to Jason before disappearing into the barn. Hank mounted up, as did Grace and Martin. Gabe led a golden mare across the corral and placed her reins in Melanie's hand. "Belle knows the trail. She'll be a good ride for you."

Thank you stuck in her throat, so all Melanie could do was nod. Belle was beautiful, all golden with white mane and tail. She stood still as Melanie set her foot in the stirrup and swung up. Gathering the reins, she sat still and watched Gabe help Jason on Nipper. Gabe whispered something that got Jason grinning, and then showed him how to hold the reins. A second later, Jason walked his horse over to her.

"Look, Mom, I'm riding a horse. All by myself! Wait until I get home and tell Robby!"

"Good job, Jay." Melanie grinned. Jason's friends were going to hear this story over and over again.

Gabe rode up on her other side. His gray gelding stood taller than hers. "All right, Bud, fall in line."

Grace and Martin led them along a wooded trail. Jason rode beside Hank. At the end of the line came Melanie and

Gabe. She tried to retain her anger, but out in the gorgeous afternoon, lulled by the steady rock of the horse and faint buzz of nuisance insects, she could only sigh.

"I thought I was a goner," Gabe muttered under his breath.

His quiet admission sent a tingle through her. The butterflies in her stomach outnumbered the ones flitting about the wildflowers a hundred to one. She bit her lip to keep from smiling.

"I thought you were, too." She kept her gaze straight ahead. "Lucky for you I'm a goner when it comes to trail rides." She snuck a peek at him and grinned. "Don't do it again."

He tipped his hat at her. "Scout's honor."

They followed a steady incline for over an hour. Pine trees as dense as thicket lined the trail. Wildflowers fringed the low-growth bushes, making them look like bouquets waiting for a wedding. When the other horses pulled to a stop, Melanie rode up beside Grace and stared into the most beautiful contrasts of nature she could've ever imagined.

Never-ending sky as blue as cobalt paint set as background to snow-tipped mountain peaks. The valley meadow below, carpeted in thick, green grasses with white and yellow flowers, added a lacy shimmer over velvety patches. Far below, a stream rumbled, the sound of rushing water bouncing up the rock walls on the other side.

Solid, majestic pines dotted the field, growing denser as they wound up hillsides until a forest of trees rimmed the land much like a frame captures and exhibits a fine painting. Tiny chipmunklike pika scurried across a cropping of moss rocks, playing in the summer sun.

Melanie rested her forearm on the saddle horn. "I've seen lots of mountain meadows, but nothing as perfect as this."

"Water company wanted to pipe along the tree line a couple of years ago." Martin removed his hat and wiped his forehead.

"Wanted to put a housing development in a few miles up the road. Said they couldn't build without water."

He put his hat back on his head and looked out across the valley. "Didn't get his water. The development didn't get built. Guess the fella knew what he was talking about."

"How do you get water, Mr. Martin?" Jason sat tall on his horse right beside the older man.

"My grandfather dug a deep well." He winked at the boy. "It ain't never gone dry."

"Enough for the horses and all the cows, too?"

"The Lord provides for everyone." He leaned back in his saddle and gave Jason a long look. "Nothing better than a summer Sunday afternoon spent fishing. What do you think, young man?"

Within an hour, after weaving their way down from the craggy overhang, around groves of aspen trees and outcroppings of moss rock, Jason held a fishing pole in his hands and bobbed the tip of the line. Serious concentration pulled his blond brows together as Martin tugged on the line and pointed out spots in the river. Gabe smiled. If he'd worried about wrecking Jason's summer with a few weeks of work here on the ranch, he should have remembered his folks and their penchant for entertaining.

The grin on his face faded.

His dad. And his mom. Both tough as leather chaps and just as durable. Long days and short nights pulling the ranch together hadn't fazed them. They just looked to each other for support and kept on plowing along.

His jaw grew tight when Nick and Zac popped into his mind. Sure, Zac did his fair share, handling the business end from Denver. The good Lord knew Gabe didn't want to go anywhere near the city for longer than a day. But Nick? How did driving cross-country, riding bulls, and banging himself up help the overall scheme of things? His wife's death had been a shock to everyone, but Nick continued to punish himself.

Gabe needed him back on the Circle D. Now. Before Gabe tangled up so many ends it would take an explosion to fix it all.

Water gurgled around the rocks beneath his feet. A drop of water spit into the air and landed on his hand. The truth of the matter boiled down to Nick and Zac grabbing their gold rings when the carousel of life had swept by. And Gabe had just watched and skipped his turn.

Don't worry. Gabe will take care of it. The familiar refrain rang through his head.

He skipped a pebble into the water, disrupting the echo of Zac's voice in his ear. Everyone just assumed Gabe would be around to keep the ranch going. He jammed his hand in his front pocket and picked his way along the river edge. Had anyone ever asked him if *he* had plans? Did he even know?

"Gabe, wanna fish?"

He ruffled Jason's hair. "Get any bites yet?"

"Mr. Martin said to keep my pole loose so the bait looks natural." He looked sideways at this line. "Do you think it looks natural?"

"Like a pro." Gabe grinned and the tension in his shoulders eased. "Fishing takes patience. Just wait. They'll bite."

"You wanna help us?" Jason scooted over to make room.

"You and Dad have the best spot along this river. How about if I go talk to your mom so she doesn't get lonely?"

Jason frowned at the tip of his pole. "I think I felt something."

"Remember, Bud." Gabe watched the tip of the pole. "Stay loose."

The boy just nodded his head.

Yes, sir. That boy needs to go fishing more often. He glanced over to the grassy area under the fringe of the ponderosa pine. Melanie smiled in their direction—whether at him or her son, Gabe wasn't certain. He didn't care, either. She wasn't mad at him anymore, and that meant more to him than all the fish in the river.

No way was he going to stop and figure that one out.

He stepped through the tall grasses. "Looks like you found the only comfy spot around."

"I've sat on enough rocks to know I want grass when it's around."

"Smart girl."

She squinted at him. "How about you?"

"Cushion sounds pretty good right now." Gabe settled on the grass beside her.

Melanie laughed. "Cool fresh air and a hard seat, or soft, sweet padding and gnats buzzing around."

He would remember her laugh well past the heat of summer. Probably into the dead of winter. Maybe clear into next spring. "I can deal with gnats."

"It's really beautiful up here."

With unconscious grace, she tucked her hair from her face exposing her dainty ear. "Beauty can be found anywhere you look."

"Hmm, I wasn't thinking philosophical." She smiled, showing straight teeth and a tiny dimple at the corner of her mouth. "I mean this is the kind of place postcards are made of."

He pulled a blade of timothy grass and stuck it in his mouth. "A lot of the National Forest in this end of the state is wooded like this. You'll have your groves of aspen fringing the pines that stretch up to the higher elevations, and then a mix of pasture or rock face just to break up the monotony."

"A postcard and the tour guide to go with it. Can't beat that."

"Yeah, well." He looked up at the cloudless sky. "I never get tired of it."

"I envy you."

Gabe turned at her wistful sigh. "Why?"

"You know what you want." She dropped her gaze and began to pick at a thread on her jeans. "You get to live it."

He coughed at *that* irony. He hadn't had much choice. "My life is what it is. You've got the best of all worlds."

She tipped her chin. "I do?"

He tipped his head toward the river where Jason stood at the edge of the water. "Yes, ma'am. He's going to grow into a fine young man with a love for bugs and the outdoors."

"Jason can't help but know bugs." Her shy laugh told him she loved every moment. "Hey, I'm the best draw on show-and-tell days at school."

"Do you bring in live examples?"

"I have the kids catch all the bugs in the playground, we sit at the tables outside and I tell them what they've found. That's the educational part. Sooner or later, some boy tosses his specimen on a girl, and then that's all she wrote."

"You mean boys still do that sort of thing?"

She scrunched her face into an *are you kidding?* expression. "That sport will go on through time as long as boys are boys and girls are girls. Only now, the girls don't hesitate to throw their bugs back at the boys."

Gabe watched his dad and Jason put their heads together as Martin pointed over the water. "Kids are great."

"Yeah, they are."

At the river, Jason stepped to the side and bobbed his pole a little more. His dad wore a grin Gabe hadn't seen in a long time. "Someday…"

The sweet smell of sage wrapped around them. Melanie shot him a look from beneath her raised brow. "Is someday very far off? Maybe with a cute strawberry blonde?"

"Hmm?"

Melanie shrugged her shoulders. "You know. From church this morning."

Strawberry blonde? Jennifer? Was that the color of her hair?

Gabe shook his head. "We've grown up together." He

thought back to school and summer breaks. "Actually she used to tag along behind Zac, but then, who didn't? The kid was a Pied Piper of trouble. I think I remember Jen getting grounded for a week helping him with some harebrained scheme. Come to think of it, lots of kids got in trouble following Zac."

"I take it you were an angel?"

"Far from it." He chuckled at the thought. "I had the common decency to keep trouble contained to family members and didn't spread misery through town."

"How noble." She tossed a pebble at him. Squared him on the stomach. Her eyes grew wide, but she threw another anyway. "So, this barbecue. Sounds like we're going to have lots of help."

"I knew you would." He tossed a pebble back. "Just consider yourself a coordinator."

She ducked the shot. "The ladies at your church all seem so nice and welcoming."

"They love visitors and they love to cook. You've provided them with both. If you want to see a feast, you should be here for the Labor Day picnic. Our country deserves all the respect we can give it, and the ladies show respect right with food."

"Maybe I'll have to put Labor Day on my schedule."

"You wouldn't be disappointed." Tables laden with pies, breads and casseroles created the most mouth-watering smells as the pastor gave his Labor Day sermon outside beside the banquet in a tent. "God does provide, and on that day we give thanks for so much."

"I'd love to—"

"Mom! I caught a fish!" Jason yelled from the riverbank. "It's huge!"

Chapter Eight

"Play it to the right." Blood pumped through Gabe's veins to rival the excitement in Jason's voice. "Keep a steady hand, Bud. That's right."

"It's stuck." He gave the pole a jerk. "I can't move it any closer."

"The fish know what rocks to hide behind. Don't worry, he won't get away."

Water splashed as the fish jumped in the air. Gabe squeezed Jason's shoulder and angled his body toward the fish. "Keep your eye on the fish."

"He's coming closer."

"Hold 'em steady," Martin directed from beside Jason. "I'll grab the line."

Jason held still, his hands locked on the pole and reel. Martin caught the taut fishing line and pulled the fish straight up out of the water. Flapping in the air, the trout refused to give up.

"He's huge." Jason angled his pole to the side. Eyes wide open, he turned to Gabe. "He's huge."

"That he is, Bud." Pride spread through Gabe. "Mighty nice fish for your first time."

"Jason." Melanie drew up close beside him, her fingers

tugging on his sleeve for balance on the smooth river rock. "That's a great catch. Let me get a picture."

Gabe leaned back to give her full view of her son and his prize. She snapped two shots. He urged her back a couple steps as water splashed over his boots. "Can we continue the photo op on dry ground?"

Her megawatt smile never faded. "Oops, sorry. Got carried away." She tucked her camera into her pocket. "C'mon Jason, let me see him."

Martin held the fish while Jason hopped to the bank, his pole still securely in his hands. "Mom! I did it. I caught a fish."

"From the looks of him, I'd say a three pounder. Nice size, Bud." Gabe joined Martin on the bank.

Martin removed the hook while Grace, Hank and Melanie congratulated Jason. Gabe couldn't have felt any prouder of him than if he'd caught a record trout himself. Jason sported a grin to split his face.

"Thanks for your help, Gabe. I'm glad he didn't get away."

"Another couple times out and you'll be a pro."

"Here, young man." Martin offered the stringer holding the fish. "Hold your trophy."

Melanie backed up. "Smile, Jason." She snapped a few shots. "I need his coaches in the picture, too." She waved to him and his dad.

Gabe took his place beside Jason, Martin on the other side. Melanie issued directions like a professional photographer. He couldn't help but grin. He hadn't enjoyed fishing this much since…he couldn't remember when. Grace and Hank joined the picture, too.

"Melanie, you get in the picture." Grace left the lineup and took the camera from Melanie. Hank and Martin moved aside. Melanie took Martin's spot next to Gabe with Jason standing between them.

She looked up at him, her blue eyes gleaming. "What a day to remember."

"Smile, you guys." Grace took the picture. She waved her hand. "Closer."

Automatically, his palm gripped her shoulder and pulled Melanie closer. Jason wiggled back, his fish held in front of him. Awareness of the cozy scene they presented shot through Gabe as he pressed the three of them together. His face heated as him mom snapped away and chattered about how great the pictures would look.

"Stop, Miss Grace," Jason whined. "My arm is tired."

Martin took the stringer from Jason. "That fish needs to go back in the water."

Grace lowered the camera. "So Jason, are we going to catch and release, or eat 'em?"

"Eat."

"All right, then." Martin headed toward the water. "We've got some work ahead of us. Can't feed the family on one fish like Jesus fed the five thousand."

Gabe kept his hand on Melanie's shoulder as Jason ran to the water edge. He urged her toward his horse.

"Where we going?" She looked up at him, confused.

He unsnapped the roll behind his cantle and pulled out the three segments of his fishing rod. "C'mon, Mom. Time for you to earn your keep."

"Doesn't matter to me, I like 'em."

"Like what?" Melanie caught the tail end of their conversation when she walked through the open door into Gabe's kitchen looking for Jason. No sooner had they returned from their ride with Martin's saddle bags filled with fish and tended to the horses, Jason took off after Gabe carrying his one fish while Gabe handled the rest. Melanie knew if she found Gabe, she'd find Jason.

She'd been surprised to find Gabe didn't live with his

parents. Surprised and oddly relieved. He'd built a house just through a stand of pine trees on the other side of the barn and corrals. Far enough away for privacy, yet close enough for emergencies.

Since he lived alone, she didn't know what to expect. A spacious kitchen lined with knotty pine cabinets, deep green and black granite countertops, and a bank of windows at the sink hadn't been on her radar. The plank wood floor added style; the gleaming pots and pans suspended over the center island added class. She looked around the room, careful to keep her mouth from falling open. Nothing resembled the clutter and mess she'd seen in the ranch office.

Now, wasn't Gabe Davidson just full of surprises?

"Fish." Jason stood on a step stool at the sink. He held up the one he'd cleaned. "You don't like fish."

She flopped her pack on the island. "Fish are okay."

"Mom wouldn't let a dead fish in her kitchen for all the money in the world." Jason ran his finger along the fish belly then placed it on top of the stack of fish they'd already cleaned. "She doesn't do slimy."

Gabe looked up from the sink. His brown eyes rimmed with thick black lashes sparkled with mischief. "They're welcome in mine. And fish aren't slimy." He scraped over the side of the fish in his hand. "These are rainbow trout. You can tell because they look like they have rainbow stripes along their sides." He handed it to Jason. "They have scales, not slime."

"They're slimy, like snakes." Jason wiggled the fish over the sink.

"Snakes aren't slimy." Melanie found her voice. Now if she could just find her breath. "They're slithery."

"So?" Jason dropped the fish on top of the others they'd already cleaned. "You don't like them, either."

Gabe claimed the next fish. "This is a strange picture I'm seeing here. You can handle insects, wasps and spiders, but not fish or snakes?"

Her cheeks warmed. "I never said I didn't like fish."

"But you don't like snakes."

"Do you?"

Gabe handled it with ease. "They're okay. They do a lot of good."

Long fingers wrapped around the fish, and the muscles of his forearms bunched with little effort. She leaned against the island and fingered her pack strap to keep from staring. "So do insects, wasps and spiders. Not too crazy about mosquitoes, but hey, fish eat them."

Jason snickered. "Good one, Mom. Watch me."

Gabe made room at the sink whether she wanted it or not. She squeezed in between them. Jason worked like a pro. "Good job, big guy."

"Yep." He finished and reached for a paper towel. He wiped his hands, a satisfied look on his face. "Gabe will teach you how to do it, too. Won't you, Gabe?"

"Sure." He reached around her and picked up the last fish. "You're in luck, we have one more."

Memories of high school biology came flooding back. She raised a brow at him in silent challenge. "Great. No problem at all."

"Here, hold the knife like this." After placing the knife handle in her right hand, he wrapped her fingers shut. "And the fish like this."

He kept his rough palm under her left hand for support. Her grip tightened around the cold trout. She nestled her knuckles into his palm.

"Now, right along here."

It had been a long time since she'd attempted simple dissections. Her life revolved around pinning insects and diagramming plants. This was going to take all day. As if reading her thoughts, Gabe gripped her bunched fist and changed her angle to underhand. "Now you have leverage."

His work-hardened hands guided her with gentle yet

decisive motion. Her palms turned clammy, whether from the fish or her nerves she wasn't certain. She did know that she hadn't been this close to a man in years.

"Ouch." The muscles in his arm jerked.

"Sorry." She pulled away. He held on tighter. What a time to daydream. She tried to drop the knife into the sink.

"Let's try again." His breath fluffed her hair.

She shook her bangs out of her eyes. Gabe chuckled in her ear. "Relax. I'm only letting you cut me once."

"Sorry." Heat flashed down her neck.

Jason drummed his fingers on the countertop. "I'm done already, Mom. You've got the last one. Hurry."

"Hey, Bud, cut your mom some slack here." The words rumbled in his chest. "You're a pro now. We've got to be patient with beginners." He chuckled in her ear again. "Slow and easy."

Voice, don't fail me now. "Maybe if I could have my hands back, I could do some work."

"After this fish."

Hands together, he led her through the steps. She paid close attention, careful not to let the knife slip. As they neared the end of the task, she worked with gusto to get the job done.

"Hey Mom, look!"

Gabe and Melanie turned at the same time. The click of the camera captured the moment. Melanie blinked at the flash as Jason lowered the camera and stood proud. "You do that to me all the time. I finally got one of you."

"Jason." Spots swam before her eyes.

Gabe's arms tightened around her, his elbows fit perfectly in the curve of her waist. She leaned back into his chest, a sturdy wall of support. Giggles filled the room. Jason held the camera to his face for another shot. Melanie hoped he would remember in years to come what they were all doing that afternoon.

Just cleaning fish…

And the one in her palm kept her from taking the camera from him. "Did you wash your hands?"

"Rubbed them on my jeans." He rewarded her with a toothy grin. "Don't worry, your camera isn't slimy."

She looked up at Gabe. His suntanned jaw and slight burn across the nose filled her vision. Tiny lines appeared in the corners of his beautiful brown eyes as thick black lashes framed his humor. If another flash of the camera hadn't disrupted her thoughts, she might have drawn closer for a better look.

Her hands remained full of fish; the knife still poised for action. "Jason Hunter, put that camera down."

"Okay." His grin grew wider as he set the camera on the island counter. "Can't wait to see these pictures on our screen saver at home."

Neither could she. She shook her head at him and a strand of hair fell across her nose. She tried to brush it off with her shoulder. Frustrated with the entire chain of events, she squinted at her son. "Can I please have a towel?"

"Here." The arms around her shifted. Gabe offered his sleeve. "Let me."

She swiped her face across his sleeve and then jerked upright, glancing around for Jason poised with the camera. All clear. "I hate it when my nose itches and I can't scratch it."

"I know exactly what you mean."

"Thanks."

His grin made his eyes shine. Melanie just stared.

"You're welcome." He lifted her hands over the counter and shook until the fish and knife dropped from her grasp. The knife clattered into the stainless steel sink. He turned on the water and handed her soap.

"Thanks, again." Her knees braced against the cabinet door to keep from buckling as she washed her hands.

"Not a problem. Glad I could help." Gabe washed his hands

and turned to Jason. "Well, these fish won't fry themselves. Why don't you help me set up the fire for grillin'?"

"You mean a barbecue?"

"No, I mean a fire pit out back. We fill it with wood, light a match and put a grill on top of it. Best way to have fresh fish."

Jason wrinkled his nose. "Well, if you say—"

"Come, young grasshopper." Gabe slid the fish into a large plastic bag. He sealed it shut as he walked over to the refrigerator and placed them on the top shelf. Attention on Jason, he nodded toward the door. "We will learn the way of fire."

Jason tracked across the room, a frown on his face. The two of them stepped through the door, Gabe explaining the concept of the pit grill. Melanie heaved out a sigh and leaned her elbows on the dark granite countertop. Her skin tingled and she ran her fingers across her cheek, afraid the last few moments would remain indelibly etched in her mind. At the sound of pounding feet, she glanced across the kitchen. Jason poked around the jamb.

"Get the frying pan on the stove," he whispered way too loudly. "I'm not sure about this plan."

Laughter from across the yard rekindled the warmth in her belly. Melanie looked out the window.

Gabe waved for Jason. "Oh ye of little faith."

Melanie stepped out of Gabe's house, snagging the handle of the screen door before it slammed into place. The natural-wood-finished porch lined with smooth pine rails wrapped around the house, the wide, shallow steps spilling into a yard filled with native grasses. A replica windmill sat in the middle of a patch of gravel, large stones arranged around it in a precise pattern.

The entire setting reminded her of the clubhouse at a mountain camp she'd attended as a teenager. Each summer she'd spent two weeks of sun and fun at the edge of a lake surrounded by fellow campers eager to swim and canoe.

Good times.

Her muscles relaxed as she wandered over to the bench swing suspended in the corner of the porch. Stained natural like the rest of the woodwork and wide enough for two. A striped cushion fixed to the back and seat beckoned her to sit. The cushion fluffed around her like a well-filled down comforter as she snuggled deep. She pushed off with one foot and the swing took up an easy sway.

A suspense thriller lay on a side table within reach, a pair of reading glasses beside the book. Cicadas hummed in the grass. Melanie sank deeper in the cushion and kept the rhythm of the swing constant with the push of her toe.

In the distance she heard Jason calling Gabe.

Her eyes grew heavy as she listened to the creak of the swing. Someday, maybe she and Jason would find a home like this.

Chapter Nine

"Hand me a couple more logs." Gabe pointed to the wooden box with a chunk of wood. He tossed the piece into the pit as he kneeled beside the low stone wall. "Can't have the fish-fry-and-marshmallow-roast fire die too quickly."

"I love marshmallows." Jason bent over the edge of the box and came up with a cut log in each hand. "You sure about this fish fry?"

Inquisitive to a fault, Jason hounded him over the logistics of a concept that seemed as simple as the dawn of time. Gabe shook his head. What did they teach these kids in school? "Not a Boy Scout, huh?"

"No." Jason wrinkled his nose. "Were you?"

"All the way to Eagle Scout." Gabe arranged the chunks of wood in the pit. "Figured if I was going to live in the mountains, I better know how to take care of things."

Jason tossed in a couple of branches and grabbed a longer stick. He jabbed at a log. "Sounds cool. Did you have badges?"

"Yep. Had to wear my uniform to school once a month." A sea of blue shirts and yellow scarves had filled the elementary school. "I had this red vest as a cub scout. As I earned my patches, my mom sewed them on. But the first time I wore the vest to school, I hadn't earned any yet. All the older kids had tons of patches. That was the day I decided I was going to earn every one."

Jason's mouth dropped open and he stared with blue eyes every bit the color of columbines in full bloom. Eyes just like his mother's. Gabe took an extra moment before looking away. Everywhere he looked, he saw Melanie—a woman he'd met only a few days earlier.

And who would be gone just as quick.

"Did you?"

Jason's persistence brought him back to the topic at hand. Now he appreciated the effort he'd put into earning the honor. Back when he'd worked on his projects, he'd wondered at his ambition. "It took years, but I did. So did my brothers. We're all Eagle Scouts."

"What does that mean?"

It means you understand your responsibilities and stick around until they're finished. Immediately, Gabe felt petty and unjust. Nick and Zac had their own lives to deal with. If he really thought about it, he'd gotten the best end of the stick, since he'd stayed on the ranch. Still, it wouldn't hurt for his brothers to check in on their folks once in a while.

Gabe stood and swiped his palm down his thigh. He caught Jason's earnest gaze and felt even smaller than he thought possible. Attaining the rank of Eagle Scout had meant work and dedication, and unselfish service to others. A trait Gabe fell short of time and again.

He knew Jason didn't want to hear about the honor others read into the title. Maybe someday, but not now. "It means I know how to start a fire and grill a few fish over the flames."

Jason poked the woodpile with the stick. "Prove it."

"Oh really? Do I hear a dare?" On the last word, Gabe lunged at Jason and caught the boy off guard. Giggles erupted as Gabe lifted Jason into his arms. The boy curled up like a bug and wiggled just as much. Gabe stood his ground, tickling wherever his fingers landed. Jason tried to squirm out of his grasp, but Gabe tossed hay bales heavier than Jason. Eagle Scout skills weren't required at the moment. "Give?"

"Uncle!" Jason hollered the age-old surrender.

"Enough?"

"For now." A large shadow passed over them. Jason looked up. "What's that?"

"A bald eagle." Gabe pointed past the open meadow to the mountain range. "They have a nest in the crags of that ridge over there."

Jason shaded his eyes and stared. "Wow."

Gabe lowered his line of sight to his house. There on the porch, Melanie sat in his swing, her head propped against the cushion, her eyes closed. His stomach did a flip and he lost track of their conversation.

The old swing never looked better.

Melanie, Grace and Martin sat in camp chairs around the pit. Jason loaded his hundredth marshmallow on the stick. Gabe stood by the fire with Jason feeding the flames and showing her son how to keep the treat at a distance from the flames to toast it, not incinerate it.

Melanie held her own stick, the white puff on the end consumed by flames. She blew out the fire, pulled the blackened skin off the marshmallow and popped it into her mouth. Nothing better than charred marshmallows.

She leaned back and fiddled with the pop-top of the soda can in the cup holder. Crickets chirped around her and cicadas buzzed in the dark. A slight breeze rustled the branches of the surrounding trees, the sweet scent of sage kissing the air. She closed her eyes and drank in the night. Peace and serenity. It had been so long, she hardly recognized it.

Gabe's gentle voice drifted from the edge of the fire pit.

Jason asked countless questions and Gabe fielded them all with patient attention. His heart for children warmed her soul.

Thank you, Lord.

Hank came out of the kitchen with mugs and a tin coffeepot in his hand. "Best coffee you'll ever taste. This pot's been through campouts, hunting camps and more than its share of evening marshmallow roasts. Here." He handed out mugs. "Now you tell me if this isn't the best."

"Thanks." Melanie accepted her mug and held it out for the evening brew. "You do it all, don't you, Hank?"

"Yes, ma'am." He held up the sugar. "Got to know how to survive in the wild, and if you don't make good coffee you're a dead man, no matter how you look at it."

She reached for the cream. "Glad to hear you plan to stick around awhile."

The conversation turned to coffee and tea, leading eventually to how good the brew depended solely on the quality of the water. The well water on the ranch was the best around. She had to admit, the water did taste crisp and fresh.

"I know what we need." Gabe turned back to the fire. "We need some music."

"That we do." Hank set the coffeepot down. "The night wouldn't be complete without campfire songs."

The two men headed toward the house as Melanie relaxed in her seat. The breeze shifted and a puff of smoke blew past her. She sniffed and sneezed.

"You okay?" Grace handed her an extra napkin.

Melanie wrinkled her nose. "Just the smell of nature." She blew her nose as delicately as possible. "I've been to church, ridden a horse, caught fish, gathered firewood, and finished the best meal I've ever had. How much better can a day get?"

"Well, how's your singing?" Martin leaned forward and tossed another log on the fire. Sparks flew all around them.

Melanie sneezed again.

"Bless you," Grace offered. "What you're saying is you've had too much fun for one day?"

"I can't remember when I've done so much in one day." She glanced at the log where Jason sat, poking the tip of a stick in the fire. So much family time.

Gabe and Hank returned, guitars in hand. The two strummed a few chords and tuned up. Then Gabe began playing in earnest. "Oh give me a home, where the buffalo roam…"

"And the deer and the antelope play." Melanie joined in as all their voices rose to the words. Hank played harmony to Gabe's melody. The guitars sounded great. She couldn't say the same for the portion she contributed. When they ran out of familiar verses, Gabe chorded to a close.

Melanie giggled. "Funny how you don't forget the words to some songs."

"Classics, my dear, classics," Gabe answered in singsong as he changed tunes. His long fingers glided over the neck of the guitar, graceful in their motion. The firelight danced in reflection off of the polished wood as the pick he held between his fingers worked over the strings. The tempo picked up.

"I come from Alabama with a banjo on my knee."

"I'm gone to Louisiana where my true love waits for me," Hank picked up while Gabe held his note. The two offered a duet that sounded suspiciously rehearsed. Melanie tapped her foot in rhythm. Best show she'd ever seen.

Jason laid his stick on the stones beside the pit. She motioned for him to step around and join her. Displaying none of the energy he'd had all day, he skirted the crowd and slid up on her lap. She gave him a squeeze and hummed along with the tune.

"Gabe and Hank play pretty good, don't they?" She rubbed her face in his hair.

"Um-hmm." Jason wiggled around until he found just the

right spot then began swinging his foot to the tune. "Wonder if he knows any Garth Brooks?"

"Did I hear a request?" In true performer spirit, Hank scanned the crowd. "Did I hear Garth Brooks?"

"Uh-huh. Know any?"

Gabe said something to Hank over his shoulder. Hank picked a couple cords. Fingers began playing the strings as the opening bars to "Rodeo" filled the air. He grinned and winked at Jason as he began describing the bucking bull in the low voice made famous by the country singer.

Jason bounced on her knees, fully awake now. He joined in as the men came to the chorus, shouting a rather off-key "Rodeo-o-o" of his own. Martin sat up and added his own flat harmony. Grace clapped her hands.

Animation colored Gabe's pitch, and the entire song became a free-for-all.

Laughing so hard, Melanie thought she'd cry.

The men strummed their final chord.

"That was great." Jason clamped his hands down on her thighs like vices. "Sing another one."

That half smile Melanie had come to search for on Gabe accompanied his humble bow. "Thank you, folks, for your appreciation of the music made by a pair of lowly cowboys. Now for something a little slower."

His fingers danced along the neck of the guitar as graceful as the hawks she'd seen the other day soaring through the air. Gabe hummed and picked at his guitar. His eyes closed, he appeared in complete worship. The tune became familiar and Melanie grew still. The words popped into her mind even before Gabe began to sing.

"Praise the name of Jesus," Gabe and Hank sang in harmony.

"Praise the name of Jesus," Grace joined in.

Martin hummed. Jason swayed.

She'd once belted out the words of the familiar song,

swayed to the music. Right beside Paul, within the singles group. They'd sung the truth from the very bottom of their souls. He'd hug her afterward and they'd all go out to lunch at a café around the corner from the church. She'd clasped on to the joy, not wanting to ever let it go.

Not thinking there was a reason.

Ahhh, how times change in the blink of an eye.

Her stomach knotted so tight her meal protested. Pain and anger rose; she tamped them down. They couldn't hurt her now. Not anymore.

Sucking in a deep breath, Melanie heard Gabe's words ring thick with praise: "He's my rock, He's my fortress…"

"In Him will I trust." The words came out of her mouth as natural as breathing. Her mouth snapped closed. She'd trusted God and fell in love with Paul. All the girls drooled over him. She'd beamed when he'd shown interest in her. They'd worshipped together, attended the singles events together, went on dates with other church couples. God had answered her prayers by bringing Paul into her life.

Jason swayed on her knees, his boyish voice singing the refrain, his shoulder movements familiar in a bizarre, déjà vu fashion. Melanie closed her eyes and saw Paul standing beside her in church singing the final hymn of the morning, his arm around her, his hand clutching the waistband of her skirt tighter than was proper.

Lies no longer tempted her. But the deceit lived on.

Her eyes snapped open, and the final chorus around the campfire wound to a close. She'd never allow herself to get hurt like that again. She kept her eyes open now.

Melanie gave Jason a squeeze and cleared her throat. "Do we have entertainment for the picnic?"

Gabe pulled the strap over his head and swung his guitar down to his side. "I think our local boys will provide the music. Hank and I will have our hands full penning cattle."

"Too bad." She collected her thoughts as Jason raved over the music.

"Well now." Grace angled and stood up. "We've a got a few nights ahead of us yet. I'm sure we'll have a chance to sing some more."

"You were great." Jason slid off Melanie's knees, allowing the blood to circulate through her legs.

"Yes, you were." Melanie stared at Gabe, her emotions raw.

Gabe tossed a chunk of bark into the glowing pit; his long lashes made even longer by firelight. His crooked smile warmed her clear down to her toes. "Thanks."

Martin stood up a bit slower than the rest of them. He rubbed circulation back into his left arm. "Time to call it a night. Work tomorrow."

Melanie stood and stretched. She lifted her chin to the black night sky dusted with crystal chips. "I have a meeting with Mrs. Wells tomorrow."

"Bright and early." Grace nodded. "You've got a party to plan and you don't have much time to do it."

"Amen," Melanie whispered under her breath. Good thing—not too much time to plan. She needed to finish her obligation fast. She rolled her head from side to side and then stole a look at Gabe, meeting his curious gaze across the low-burning fire.

Looks like that had gotten her in trouble before. Hadn't she just relived the moment? She turned away and reached for Jason, almost pulling him toward the path leading back to their cabin.

The next morning, Melanie trudged toward the ranch house. The connection with Gabe she experienced the night before unsettled her. Thankfully, she'd be spending the day with Grace and the ladies making menu plans. Jason had left a few minutes earlier, intent on finding leftovers from breakfast.

The pickup stood in front of the house. Embarrassment rose as she remembered the muddy mess she'd made of herself and Gabe the day she'd met him. She rounded the truck bed and found RJ leaning against the door.

"Mornin', ma'am. Fine day for a drive to church."

Handsome in his own right, this lanky cowboy brought to life all that was country, from his worn boots to his crumpled hat. He made her smile with his own brand of laid-backness, but that was as far as attraction went.

She had her hands full with the tingle she experienced whenever Gabe walked up. "Good morning, RJ. Have you seen Jason? I don't want to make Grace wait."

"Just a second ago." He pointed toward the kitchen.

Heads bobbed beyond the kitchen window. "Hey, Jason. Let's go."

Jason ran out of the house. "Miss Grace had biscuits left for me." He ran past her to the truck.

"Is Grace coming?"

"She'll be by to pick us up." Jason wiped his hands on his jeans. "Hey, RJ."

Melanie cringed at the thought of facing the planning committee by herself. A butterfly flitted around the wildflowers edging Grace's yard, their tiny blue blossoms stretching in the sunlight. So how unruly could a group of church ladies get?

"Emma Jean, the tomatoes aren't anywhere near ripe yet. No one will want to eat that salad." Frannie Pollard shook her head.

"I will, and so will my boys."

"Only because you tell them they have to."

"Do not!" Emma Jean Cisco glared at Frannie. "Everyone expects my tomato salad on the menu. This year I'm making a double batch."

"Ladies, please." Mary Wells clapped her hands together. "There will be room on the tables for all your delicious dishes."

Feeling more like a parent aid in one of the elementary school classes rather than an event coordinator, Melanie stood up. "I haven't checked yet, but I'm certain to find enough tables to hold all the wonderful dishes you plan on preparing."

Mrs. Wells spread her arms to continue the pacification. "Of course we'll be able to offer all the tasty dishes everyone brings."

"If everyone don't come down sick after eating green tomatoes," Frannie Pollard mumbled just loud enough.

Before pencils starting flying across the table, Melanie turned to Emma Jean. "If you'd like, I'd be happy to create place cards with your name and the name of your dish. It will follow a firecracker theme."

"Say, that does sound nice." Emma Jean sat back in her chair and grinned. "You're doing a fine job of bringing this picnic together, Melanie."

Melanie gave her thanks and sat down while Mrs. Wells went on with the plans for decorating, seating and everything else associated with the event. Melanie wanted to kiss her. She had no idea so much went into a simple barbecue.

A menu of slow-roasted barbecue beef, salads, rolls and desserts came together.

"How about pork ribs?" Melanie glanced around the room. "I have my uncle's secret recipe for the best pork rib you've ever tasted."

Mrs. Wells dropped her pencil on the table. "We live in cattle country. We'll eat what the land provides us."

"Mrs. Wells, beef is always our number one choice," Jennifer O'Reilly piped up. "Traditions don't disappear with new ideas. If folks like it, we'll say you thought of it. If they hate it, we'll say it was all Melanie's idea."

Melanie snapped around and glared at the woman she thought was her friend.

Jennifer winked at her. "You'll be long gone by then. Easy to dump blame that way."

"Jennifer O'Reilly, no one will be blamed. We will discuss the merits of the idea and decide next meeting."

Confused by the democratic process adapted by the good folks of Hawk Ridge, Colorado, Melanie's thoughts continued to jumble together as everyone gathered their papers and the chatter of excitement over the upcoming picnic drifted out the back door. She fingered her pad of paper and cleared her throat. "Three weeks sounds like a short time to pull this event together."

Jennifer rolled her eyes. "They never make anything easy. But wait until you see the end results. Small wonder Gabe delegated his assignment to innocent bystanders."

"It's more like indentured servitude, but hey, I'll be able to drive back home as a direct result." Melanie couldn't help but like Jennifer. "Thanks for the support."

"Someone has to bring this town into the twenty-first century. Having you here just helps my cause." Green eyes brightened. "So, Gabe mentioned you're looking for a job?"

Melanie nodded. "In research and field work. I want a job that lets me spend more time with Jason."

"Good for you. I went to school for nursing and then came back to help in Dad's clinic." Jennifer paused a moment. "Sometimes it's depressing to think that's all there is."

Melanie bent over and picked up a paper from the floor. "All there is to what?"

"Life." Jen shrugged. "Grow up, go to school, go to work, get married, have babies, do the PTA duty and live the rest of your life wondering what you've missed."

Melanie glanced at the page and tossed it into the wastebasket. "What do you think you've missed?"

"I don't know. I love it here in Hawk Ridge, but I can't help but think God has greater plans for me."

Melanie didn't want to get into the whole "God and His

plans" thing. At one time, she thought she had that all figured out, too. "Is there something you'd like to do?"

"Lots of things."

"Well, now is the time to make those dreams come true." She dusted off her soapbox of tough choices. "I knew I needed something better than the job I had or I'd grow old and realize I'd missed Jason growing up. Change isn't easy when you're the sole breadwinner. Take your chances while you can. Plenty of time to rock on the porch when you're old."

A smile a mile wide brightened Jennifer's face. "I'm glad you understand."

Melanie understood more than Jennifer would ever realize. Taking chances with the help and support of a loving family created options when faced with hard decisions. A person grew up fast when faced with providing for themselves and an infant as their only course. She didn't recommend that route to anyone. "I haven't heard the boys in a while. Do you know where they went?"

Jen wiped her hands on a dishtowel and nodded toward the door. "Probably out back by the swing."

The swing. Her heart beat faster. "That death trap?"

Jen angled her chin, puzzled. "The swing out back? No one's ever gotten hurt on it."

Marching around the side of the church, Melanie followed the back wall until she reached the tree. The boys hollered up a storm, a boy younger than Jason twirled around on the rope. Jen came up beside her and touched her arm. "Watch, I'll show you. Hey boys, my turn!"

Jennifer walked up to the swing just as the rope came to a stop. She took a hair band from the pocket of her shorts and tied her hair into a ponytail. Helping the little boy off the plank, Jen sat down and grabbed hold of the ropes. "All right Toby, give me a shove!"

Toby and Jason pushed, sending her flying into the air. They ran back out of the way as she swooped back and forth, her ponytail swept the ground as momentum sent her in a high arc. When the swing crested over the ridge wall, she let go and sailed through the air.

Heart pounding in her throat, Melanie took off running, patting her back pocket for her phone to call 911. She fell to her knees at the edge of the drop-off and heard chatter below. Toby and Jason were on either side of Jen, all of them squealing on a huge green-tarp-covered pile of mattresses.

"It's just like a trampoline, Mom." Jason bounced until he tumbled into Toby. "Com'ere and try."

There was no bottomless pit, no free fall of death. Once in the pit, the edges made a bowl out of the mountain shelf, the bottom and sides lined with foam.

Gabe was right. Remembering her tirade yesterday, she wanted the rock mountain to open up and swallow her whole. She'd formed her opinion of the situation without even checking out his explanation. Were all her decisions regarding Jason made with the same small-mindedness?

Digging her fingertips into the hard earth, she drew a breath and turned toward the swing. "All right, everyone. Move out of the way."

Jen, Jason and Toby scrambled to the side as Melanie sat down on the seat and grabbed hold of the rope. She pushed off with her toe.

"Don't worry, I'll give you a push." The little boy she'd seen before pushed against her back until he ran beneath her seat and let gravity swing her back. Air rushed past her ears and scent of warm pine air filled her senses. She pointed her face to the wind and closed her eyes, conscious of the creak in the trees beside her and the stout ropes clenched within her grip.

Voices ebbed and flowed around her. "Mom, let go."

Melanie opened her eyes. A whirl of pine needles and blue sky rushed past. Swinging back toward the trees, she loosened her hold. As blue sky surrounded her again, she let go.

She sailed through the air, her arms and legs kicking at nothing.

After a lifetime suspended in a moment, she landed on the loose tarp, the mattresses beneath absorbing the fall.

Wow.

Jason stuck his head over the edge and looked down at her. "Are you all right?"

Sprawled out on the tarp, she grinned at him. "Let's do that again."

Chapter Ten

Mentally adding up the hours in the day, Gabe still couldn't make heads or tails of his workload. Check the north range cattle, shoe horses, Ditch Witch the main irrigation…the list faded into eternity.

Yet here he sat in front of the church.

He turned off the engine of the truck and stretched his neck muscles until a joint popped. Wrist atop the steering wheel, he wiggled a finger as he thought up more chores waiting for him.

The memory of his dad hunched atop his stool, burning the midnight oil as he worked leather, smacked Gabe upside the head. His dad had built up the ranch with only Uncle Bob to help. How could Gabe complain about too little time and too few resources when all he had to do was check cattle and finish paperwork? Zac managed the assets; Nick worked PR…sort of. All Gabe had to do was tend this little chunk of land.

Come to Me all ye who are weak and heavy laden….

The familiar verse from the Sunday sermon wove through his mind like twenty-pound test line. This wasn't a heavy burden. This was frustration. Frustration over having too much to do and not enough time in the day to do it right.

Grabbing the keys from the ignition, he swung the door open and stepped out. The sun warmed the top of his head before he slapped on his hat. He wasn't about to waste a day in self-pity when the good Lord had just answered his biggest prayer. Melanie running herd on the ladies gifted Gabe with the time he needed. An hour or two spent making sure his help stayed happy didn't begin to empty the coffers of his appreciation.

Nope. Not one bit. He stepped up on the stoop and opened the door.

"Hello, ladies." The kitchen stood empty. His grin faded. He poked his head into the all-purpose room. Empty. RJ said he'd dropped them off. Gabe paced through the rest of the church. Nothing.

Through the window, he could hear children squeal in the backyard. He retraced his steps and headed toward the kitchen and out the door, skirting a sandbox and jungle gym at one end of the playground that kept the younger set happy.

The older kids stood around the swing tree, encouraging someone down in the pit. Gabe chuckled as Ben caught the swing and tethered it in place. That simple swing offered more enjoyment in its two stout ropes and simple seat than all the mechanized play sets in the world.

His chuckle stalled in his throat as Melanie climbed over the edge. She swatted at the dirt on her jean shorts and patted her shirt into place. Light bounced in her eyes as she shook her hair back. "Okay, boys, who's next?"

Gabe couldn't believe his ears. Melanie had tried the swing? What had happened since yesterday morning?

"You were great. Almost as graceful as Jason." Jennifer stepped up and brushed pine needles and twigs off of Melanie's backside. "Want to try it again?"

"I don't want to hog all the fun."

"We can swing anytime," Jennifer reassured her. "Go ahead. Try again."

The grin of pure joy on Melanie's face almost brought Gabe to his knees. Not a hint of fear lined her face and her smile radiated. She reached for the rope and climbed aboard.

"Okay, Jay. Give me a push."

Not one to let the moment pass him by, Gabe came up behind Jason and put his finger to his lips. The boy giggled and moved aside. Melanie flew back toward Gabe, her hair a golden mass in the sunshine. He caught her back and pushed her off. She kicked her legs and gained height. One more time, she sailed back. Gabe spread his palms around her waist, her cotton shirt soft against his skin. Silky hair threaded through his fingers and the scent of lemons teased as he pushed her back into the air.

Her body twisted and her eyes grew wide as she caught sight of him. She flew back toward him. "Gabe! This is great!"

"I know." He caught her hip and palmed her back into the air. "Look out over the ridge."

Her chin tucked to her chest, she swung upward. "Wheeeeee."

Gabe shoved her back toward the clouds; his joy surged at the freedom of the simple act.

"Let go, Mom," Jason instructed like an old pro.

Melanie swept up into the sky and released the rope just as the swing reached its zenith. She flew upward for a moment longer, then dropped to the ground with all the grace of a sack of peanuts.

"What a ride." She bounced on the cushion. "Closest I'll ever come to flying without a plane."

Gabe dropped to his belly and peered over the side. "Having fun?"

"The best." She squinted into the sun. "What a blast."

"I'm glad." Glad to see her relax; glad to see her let loose; glad to see her smile. "This swing has quite the reputation around here."

"Oh, really?" She twirled around on the cushion and crawled over to him. "What does it do?"

Gabe stared into the most incredibly blue eyes he'd ever seen. A blush of pink from the sun settled on her cheeks and a smattering of light freckles dusted over her delicate nose. He swallowed and tried to find his voice. "It makes people throw caution to the wind."

A light sparked in her eye and he thought he saw her wink. "Me? Throw caution to the wind? Not in a million years."

Yep, he'd seen the wink. "Forgive me for my misinterpretation of the moment."

Her blush deepened as her lashes lowered and her chin tilted low. "It *was* fun."

"Hey, Melanie." Jennifer stood on the other side of the pit. "You got some great air."

Tension dissolved from between his shoulders as she shifted away from the edge and stood up. Brushing the debris from her shorts and shirt, Melanie grinned at him. Jennifer ran up.

"Did you see her, Gabe?" Jen flopped down beside him. "Her second time on the swing and already a pro."

Balanced on his knees, Gabe offered Melanie a hand. She latched on and scrambled out, her fingers warm in his palm. Gray dirt sifted beneath her foot as she hopped up onto the grassy edge.

Jennifer rose and pulled a pine needle off Melanie's shorts. "Zac used to push me in the swing. I'd get just as high." She swung her hands back and forth then held them high. "I'd let go, certain I'd fly off the edge. But I never did." Her arms slapped against her sides. "I'd just land and then beg for him to do it again."

Melanie caught her breath. "I've got to do that again."

Gabe locked gazes with Melanie and couldn't tear away. His insides churned. Another turn on the swing and he'd be in heaven, too.

With timing that couldn't be beat, Jason ran up and wrapped his arms around her. "You were great!" He turned toward Gabe. "My turn. Will you push me, Gabe?"

Gabe nodded. Melanie looked away and broke the spell between them. She ruffled Jason's hair.

"Okay. Just once." She glanced back again with a shy smile. "Then my turn."

All Gabe could do was nod.

Melanie meandered through the fringe of foliage lining the acreage behind the barns. Sweet air breezed around her. She squeezed her eyes shut and filled her lungs. At times over the past twenty-four hours she'd almost been able to shake the sensation of Gabe's gentle touch as he'd pushed her in the swing.

Almost.

"Careful where you step around here. Plenty of places to twist an ankle."

Her sweet reminiscing vanished in a heartbeat. Opening her eyes, she found RJ standing beside the wheel of the tractor. The puzzled look on his face told her he'd caught her daydreaming.

"Thanks for the warning." She regained composure. "There's so much to explore around the barn and buildings. Don't know what belongs to the Davidsons and what doesn't."

He pushed away from the tractor with an easy shove and tipped back his hat. "You can walk for hours in any direction and you'll still be on the Davidson spread." He pointed all around. "They own the flats up here, most of the valley around the lake." With his thumb, he indicated behind him. "They own this whole mountain."

Did people own mountains? Melanie stared out over the flats and remembered the ride they'd taken up the slope. Martin had mentioned a developer needing water. No wonder they couldn't build. Not if the Davidsons owned miles of acreage surrounding the lake. "That's a lot of land."

"Yes, ma'am." He nodded. "But a nicer family you'll never meet. Thoughtful, too. Gabe stops by the barn every night to see how Manny is coming on the repair of your truck. Don't worry about nothing. They'll make sure your truck is as sound as any of the horses on the place."

Every night? From her cabin window she could see the light in the ranch office. Something told her it stayed on well after hers turned off. "I wish they wouldn't go to all that trouble."

"I don't believe Gabe sees it as trouble."

She gave RJ a halfhearted smile. Everything about this trip had become trouble. Funny, she couldn't quite call it an inconvenience anymore. Now that worried her more than anything else.

Beyond the shining tractor and matching mower, a trail snaked up the mountainside. Melanie stepped toward it. "Well, I'm glad I won't trespass onto some other ranch. Thanks for the chat, RJ."

"You plannin' on hiking up the side of this mountain?"

"Just a little way. I won't be gone long."

"Don't get lost. Easier to do than you think."

"I'll be careful." It couldn't be that tough to find her way around. First she'd go up, then come down. The laws of gravity had never done her wrong yet.

She picked her way along the path worn through the thick brush. Jagged rocks poked out of the carpet of pine needles, and pine boughs hung low ahead of her. Every so often, she'd stop and listen to the melody of larks and jays, and the lazy hum of flies.

The warmth of the sun heated the blend of fragrances. She took a deep breath of the rich, earthy air. Excitement rose as she fingered a patch of spongy moss on a rock beside her.

This was what she'd gone to school for—to study creation in all its natural beauty.

Lord, You've outdone Yourself with the beauty of the Rocky Mountains.

At the top of the ridge, blue sky framed layer upon layer of barren mountaintops. She maneuvered around a large rock and found a comfortable spot at the base. Below her, a small barn and pens bordered the edge of the fire pit. She recognized Gabe's house. The memory of the taste of grilled fish and roasted potatoes renewed her appetite. All the ordinary food had tasted extraordinary that night. The entertainment hadn't been bad, either.

She nestled back and stared at the green metal roof capping the log house, a smile teasing the corner of her mouth. A wet fish in one hand and the awkward handle of the knife in the other…Gabe's solid palm wrapping around her grip, guiding her as she cleaned the fish…his strong chest supporting her.

She frowned and took a breath, this time to clear her head. Succulent beef ribs, chilled macaroni salad and hot apple pies. She closed her eyes and concentrated on the picnic tastes melding together until the clean scent of summer sunshine on a cotton shirt penetrated her defenses.

"Keeping an eye on me?"

Melanie screamed, sending an echo through the valley beyond. She clutched her chest as she twisted around. "Don't sneak up on me like that!"

Gabe eased beside her and sat on a smaller rock. "I didn't sneak. I made enough noise to scare every whitetail and muley away for a mile."

"Lost in my thoughts, I guess." Her palm flattened over her pounding heart. "Sorry."

"You shouldn't be walking off by yourself. You'll get lost. Deer and elk aren't the only critters up here."

Melanie glanced over her shoulder. The well-defined trail she'd followed up didn't seem to exist any longer. Not wanting to confess she'd imagined herself above the cardinal rule of responsible mountain hiking, she nodded toward his house. "I see help."

"Umm, you and the mountain goats." The casual shrug he gave her sent tingles skittering up her back. He stretched out to the side and selected a pinecone. "Nothing prettier than summer in the Rockies. Jason enjoying his vacation?"

"Better than I'd hoped." It was true. Since they'd become involved in the ranch, Jason hadn't played his video games but a couple times. And those times had been with Gabe. "He's living the dream of any boy. I appreciate you and your family making him feel welcome."

Gabe frowned. "Don't you feel welcome?"

I don't even want to go there. "I appreciate you fixing my truck."

"Small price to pay for a party planner on such short notice." He picked at the pine needles stuck to the cone. "Having Jason around has been great. I hope we haven't put *you* out too much."

Melanie looked into the depths of his gorgeous, root-beer-colored eyes—something she'd been avoiding since yesterday. She didn't want to admit she'd had fun on the swing. She tilted her head and gave what she hoped appeared a careless shrug.

"If Jason has a great time, so do I. The only thing I'm worried about is his disappointment after the barbecue. Life back home pales compared to the cowboy life he's living." Her gaze roamed around the mountain range before her—better that than the cowboy at her side. "This is going to be a tough act to follow."

"Didn't mean to make things difficult."

The gentle warmth in his voice rammed a timber in her defenses. She forced a smile. "You didn't. You've given Jason memories he'll cherish for a lifetime."

He tilted his chin and grinned. "And you?"

She raised her hands in helpless effort. "Well, if I ever get tired of classifying plants, I guess I can always go into catering."

"My pleasure, ma'am. Glad we could expand your horizons." The corner of his mouth lifted and the killer crease in his cheek deepened. "We'd hate to have you go home empty-handed."

Joy faded at the mention of home. She would leave empty-handed, but not the way he meant. The richness and fullness of Hawk Ridge wasn't something you stumbled across every day of the week. She thanked the Lord for the gift of a few weeks.

Gabe tossed the cone with a flick of his wrist. "So, what's life like in Colorado Springs?"

"Pretty mundane. I catalog plants for research, and then assemble materials for the guys to work with and write reports to back our findings." Her life didn't interest her. His did. "How about you? Is ranching enough to tide you over for this lifetime?"

Gabe studied her with his gentle gaze. "It's a family project." He shifted his shoulders until his back leaned against her rock and his elbow rested beside her knee. "Dad has had his hands full with the place for close to fifty years. He knows every inch of the pasture, timber and hills. I've watched him my entire life and pray I'll be as good as him when he's ready to sit back and relax."

Gabe spoke with such admiration for his father. She scuffed her foot along the edge of the rock, sending pebbles dancing down the smooth surface. Gabe wanted to make his folks proud.

She'd done nothing for her parents but bring shame.

"Good for you." She gave silent thanks her voice didn't catch.

"Maybe. Maybe not." He tapped a small stone against the larger rock. Flakes of moss danced with each strike. The muscles in his forearm stood out as he gripped the stone and flicked it halfway down the rock face before it struck the ground. "I'm doing what I want to do. Sometimes I wonder if it's enough."

"How do you mean?"

"People come and go, market prices fluctuate, ranching practices are refined, yet the Circle D doesn't change. It's hard to explain." He tossed another pinecone down the hill. "Stability is probably a good thing."

"What would you like to change?"

He angled his chin and looked at her. Stared deep and long without blinking. Melanie wished she could read his thoughts. For the first time in years, she wished she could open up and offer a man more than simple surface placation. She wished she could summon the courage to crawl right in under his skin to encourage, confide, maybe even unite. Her heart pounded in anticipation, and when he looked away—when he broke the fragile connection—she deflated.

"I don't know. Maybe I'm looking for something that doesn't exist." He reached around the rock and twisted to get a good foothold and pulled himself up. "We better get back before they send search parties out after us."

He offered his hand. She accepted the help, his palm engulfed her hand to her wrist. She scrambled from her perch, not fearing in the least that she'd fall over the ridge. He steadied her while she hopped to the ground and then released her, his fingertips sliding over her knuckles.

"I know it's bad manners for a man to precede a lady, but for safety's sake, follow me. I'll be a lot softer to land on than a tree stump if you slip and fall."

She searched his face for traces of mockery. No one thought of her as a lady, much less showed concern for her safety. She couldn't remember the last time a man held a door open for her.

"Glad you know your way down from here," she puffed.

"I've traipsed up and down this mountain a thousand times."

He took off ahead of her and picked a trail down the mountain, his broad shoulders dipping with each confident step. Melanie tried to watch her steps, but her gaze insisted his well-worn jeans and crisp cotton shirt were far more enticing, not to mention the wave of thick hair at his collar.

The ranch house came in sight. Melanie shook away her wayward thoughts of gallant cowboys and handsome ranchers. Instead she concentrated on the soft crunch of pine needles beneath her every step, the cloud of gnats buzzing around her ears, the wayward splotch of sunshine heating her face. Gabe stopped at the bottom of the trail and offered her help over a fallen log. His small courtesies touched her heart.

A screen door slammed in the distance. Hank raced across the drive toward them. "Gabe. Quick! It's your dad."

Chapter Eleven

How long does it take to run a few tests? Melanie checked her watch again. Two hours and twenty-six minutes since they'd rushed Martin into the emergency room. Didn't the doctors have any information to share with them?

"Mom?" Jason sat beside her in the waiting room, a knife in one hand and a chunk of wood in the other. "Mr. Martin is going to be all right, isn't he?"

His fingers manipulated the small blade, carving a precise groove along a natural vein. Martin had given Jason that knife. Melanie swallowed to loosen the lump in her throat. "I hope the doctors come and tell us soon."

He blew off the dust he'd created and examined his work. "Hank?" Jason leaned to his other side and held out his project. "Did I do this right?"

Tight lines bracketed his mouth as Hank offered a lopsided smile. "You're a fast learner. Mr. Martin will be proud of you."

Jason never took his eyes off of the block of wood. "I want to make this for Mr. Martin. He showed me how to whittle."

A muscle twitched in Melanie's cheek. Whittle. Over the course of a week, her son had gone from city smart to country wise. Ever since the older man had taught Jason to fish, he'd followed Martin all over the ranch. In the evening before bedtime, Jason couldn't wait to share his day with her, every sentence containing any number of names he obviously respected. Especially Mr. Martin.

Melanie glanced at her watch again. Five minutes. Grace sat across the room, her head bowed in prayer. Gabe stood at the window, his shoulder propped against the mullion and arms crossed over his chest. He just stared out the glass.

Looking lost.

She folded her hands and bowed her head. Almost before her eyes closed, her mind stilled. Peace washed over her. *Lord, comfort these people. Especially him.*

An elbow poked her in the side. She opened her eyes and saw Jason frowning at her. "Mom, don't fall asleep."

She reached out and smoothed back his blond hair. "Just thinking."

His frown lifted and his shoulders relaxed. "You were grinning."

"I was looking for a happy place."

"The ranch is a pretty happy place."

She lifted her eyes and looked across the room at Gabe. "I think it is, too, honey."

Gabe shifted his weight and settled beside the window. Chin tucked into his shirt collar, he stared with a vacant look.

Unable to sit a moment longer, she walked over to him, reached out and touched his arm. "C'mon, let's walk."

Stark pain reflected in his brown eyes. She slid her hand down his sleeve and into his rough palm. As his fingers interlocked with hers, the sharp edge in his gaze softened. Melanie gave a feeble smile, the best she could manage at the moment, and tugged on his hand.

He followed her out of the waiting room. The late afternoon

air cooled her skin and cleared her head. "I love the evenings up here. The day wrapping up and getting ready for bed."

They strolled in silence, their shoulders bumped as they followed the path that meandered around the commons area of the medical-center-slash-hospital-slash-clinic. The range of medical care available in such a tiny community surprised her as she'd passed it earlier in the week. Now with Martin's health in question, she thanked the health facility for being well staffed. She pressed her knuckles into his palm, savoring the warmth of his skin. They finished the entire loop and started a second.

"I like watching the sun come up." Gabe spoke in a bare whisper beside her.

So did she. "Best part of the day."

"You've got the whole day to work, and sometimes you work into the night." The heels of his boots clicked on the cement walk, his pace easy to keep up with. "It's all gotta get done."

She loved the sound of his soft, strong voice. Even in the midst of a crisis, he maintained an even tone, a gentle calm. "I imagine there's a lot to do to keep a ranch the size of the Circle D organized."

"Cattle, hay, fence, equipment—it all needs attention. Dad knows how to do it all."

She stole a peek, the brim of his hat cast a shadow across his cheek making the lines at his eyes appear deep. "You run the place, too."

"Right now, I can't think of a thing to do."

"There isn't anything more important than being here for your family."

Gabe shook his head. "Dad wouldn't have let a little thing like someone getting sick stop him from finishing chores. Zac came down with pneumonia one winter. We all stood around his hospital bed praying for the fever to break. Waiting.

Finally, Dad had enough. He told Mom the cattle needed feed. He took Nick with him and told me to stay with Mom so she wouldn't have to drive home by herself. Dad didn't shirk responsibility."

He looked straight down as they followed the path, the very bleakness of his words etched on his face. "I can't think of a single chore that needs to be done."

Melanie squeezed his fingers and rubbed her shoulder against his sleeve. "Your dad hates feeling helpless. He needs to fill time with physical activity. He needs to fix it. Not everyone is like that." She stepped closer beside him. "Offering comfort with your presence is a gift you have. Gabe, you're a different man than your dad."

A growl rumbled deep within his chest. "You got that right."

"It's not a bad thing. When your dad is out of danger, you'll collect your thoughts and finish what needs to be done." She nudged him. "I'm sure whatever chore you think of will still be waiting for you when you're ready."

He leaned closer. "You're right. No one's racing to go muck out stalls for me."

"No, but people like being around you."

He threw her a sideways glance. "Do you?"

"Sure."

"Why?"

Why? She'd been asking that same question for days now. She walked along the path, careful not to step on the lines, a childhood habit. Why did she look forward to seeing him in the morning, or talking to him throughout the day, or wanting him to push her on the swing again just to feel his touch? Why did she trust him with her son?

Why did she want to trust him with herself? "You make me feel safe."

Steps slowed and he came to a stop. His eyes grew round as he tipped back his hat and stared at her. "Safe?"

Her cheeks burned as she scrambled to call back the truth she'd unwittingly blurted. "Well, you are a stranger after all."

"Hard to remember that." He rubbed his thumb over her knuckles. "Seems like you've been here longer than a week."

She took a step back. He held firm and tugged her closer. A surge of panic raced through her until she recognized the vulnerability in his rich, dark eyes. "This has turned into the most bizarre vacation I've ever experienced."

She wanted to bury her face in his shoulder, to feel his arms wrapped around her. She wanted to hug and be hugged in return. To offer comfort more than words. She wanted to know what safe and trust really felt like.

"Gabe! There you are!" The frantic tone of Jennifer's voice from the front doors of the emergency room cut the air. She ran down the sidewalk toward them, her white lab coat fastened by one button. "I just heard about your dad. I was in the clinic. Oh Gabe, I'm so sorry!"

Melanie snatched her hand from his, her sense of caution returning in full force. Her palm tingled as she jammed her hand in her pocket. She stepped aside as Jennifer drew closer.

Gabe opened his arm and Jennifer plowed into his chest. Her arm snaked around and caught Melanie, drawing the three of them together. Melanie folded in, her cheek pressed to Gabe's chest. Jennifer tightened them into a huddle.

"Jen, he's okay." Gabe wrapped his arm around Melanie to steady them all.

"A heart attack isn't anything to sneeze at."

Melanie snapped alert at the mention of this news. "Is he all right?"

Jennifer sniffed and turned in Gabe's arm, her slender fingers pinched his sleeve as she nodded. "My dad was still at the clinic when Sandy in Emergency called. The initial tests show Martin has some blockage. I guess he's had symptoms for a while." She blew her nose in a tissue clutched in her other hand. "It could have been so much worse."

"Could have been, but it's not." Melanie surprised herself as she offered encouragement. These lives mattered to her. She belonged here, at this moment, in this place.

Ever since she'd revealed her pregnancy, her folks, Paul, her church family...everyone had abandoned her.

She hadn't belonged anywhere.

Until now. Gabe, his parents, the community—they all believed in her. They cared.

Gabe slid his hand up to her shoulder. She wrapped her arm around his waist and leaned into his strength. She caught a glimpse of his tired sigh, his eyes moist beneath lowered lashes.

She cared about them, too.

"My dad's a tough old bird." The words rumbled in his chest. "He'll be chopping wood again before the end of the summer."

Jennifer lifted her gaze and nodded at Melanie. "I called the prayer team. Julie and Keith are coming over to the hospital." She angled her face toward Gabe. "Have you talked to your brothers?"

"I haven't had a chance. I'll call them as soon as I know Dad's all right."

"We haven't seen Zac in a long time." Jennifer pulled away from Gabe and wiped her nose. "It'll be good to see him again. And Nick."

Gabe kept his other arm draped over Melanie's shoulders. Jennifer started back toward the waiting room. Melanie leaned her head into the crook of his elbow and studied the shadow stubble along his jaw. "What a relief for you and the family to have your brothers' help."

Gabe tensed the muscles in his arm and touched his forehead to hers. "I'll call 'em. Don't hold your breath waiting for them to come."

* * *

Melanie followed the paved walkway up to the ranch office. The noisy chatter of mountain finches chirped from the trees as she brushed past the boughs. Stepping onto the deck, she knocked on the jamb, since the door already stood open. "Can I come in?"

Gabe motioned to her from behind his desk as he leaned back in his chair, the phone receiver pressed to his ear. Papers and folders cluttered his office. She picked her way to the chair he indicated and sat down. Gabe *um-hum*med into the phone as his gaze followed her every move.

"It's a heart attack, Zac. Not a stroke." Gabe rolled his eyes. "Jennifer said they ballooned his arteries and he's fine. He'll be slow for a while. That'll be the hard part."

She smiled at the assessment. Martin did tend to run the show. He'd have to take a backseat to the action until he healed.

"I can't get a hold of Nick. He must be out of cell phone range. Just come up for a weekend. Mom'll be glad to see you and Dad—well, Dad will appreciate the effort." He tapped his finger on the arm of his chair. "Of course we have enough help for the summer."

He winked and Melanie blushed. The corner of his mouth lifted, exposing white teeth. "More help than we've ever had." His grin faded as he shook his head. "Yeah, well. Of course I'll tell them."

Gabe replaced the receiver on the phone pad and stretched his neck, the strain of the last few days a shadow beneath his eyes. He rubbed the back of his neck with his hand and gave her a sideways glance. "Have any brothers and sisters?"

She shook her head. "Only child."

"Hmm. In times like this, count yourself lucky." He sat up and leaned toward the desk. "My little brother pulls the helpless card whenever there's work around here."

"He's not coming up to see your dad?"

"Oh, he'll be up, just not when we need him." Gabe placed

his elbows on the desktop, his shirtsleeves rolled to the tops of his forearms. Corded muscles flexed each time he pressed his fingers together.

Tearing her attention away from his tan skin, she looked around the office. "You have your hands full here. Isn't there some way he can come up to help?"

Gabe laughed. He propped his chin in his palm and considered her with a long look. "Nick and Zac do whatever they want to in life and face the consequences of their own decisions. Same with me. Honestly, I don't want them coming up to help me. They get in the way and then we argue." He tilted his head, the crease in his cheek deepening. "If Mom or Dad calls them, they'll come running."

She'd never understood the entire sibling rivalry issue. As an only child, she'd dealt with life alone in a big house while her father closed deals at the golf course and her mother kept a busy social calendar. She would have welcomed a sister or brother to alleviate the loneliness. "You do it all, don't you?"

"There's nothing to it. Dad grumbles. Mom makes a fuss. I watch hay grow and keep track of cattle." He ran his hand across his desk surface. "And plow through paperwork, hoping I can find all the little receipt stubs."

Melanie looked around. The desk really was a mess. As were the floor and all the horizontal surfaces in the room. If she had to keep track of files and spreadsheets in a space like this, she'd have gone crazy.

The thought nibbled at the back of her mind for all of a few seconds. A smile spread across her face. The ladies of the planning committee had the party plans well in hand, just like Gabe promised they would. Melanie had learned a lot after only a week. But organization? Now there was something she understood. "Gabe, I've got a proposition for you…"

On Thursday, the hospital discharged Martin with strict orders to exercise and watch his diet. Gabe pulled the truck up to the front yard gate as his mom waved from the kitchen door. He shifted into gear and turned off the engine. "C'mon, Dad, the welcoming committee is waiting."

He glanced over at his dad, surprised at how much he'd aged in just a few days. Tanned and rugged from living outdoors his entire life, Martin Davidson now sported hospital pallor. His cheeks thin and dark circles rimmed his eyes.

Gabe removed the keys. "I'll grab your bag."

Fletcher met them at the base of the drive, tail waggin'. Gabe got out of the truck and shut the door. After a couple of steps toward the fence gate, he heard the passenger side open. Releasing a breath, Gabe started toward the flagstone path.

Grace appeared on the porch, her hands planted on her hips.

"Gabriel Thomas Davidson, why aren't you helping your father?"

"Because his father doesn't need any help." Martin turned the corner of the pickup bed. "I ain't no invalid."

Gabe winked at his mom. She held her stance. "I have his bag. What else should I do?"

"Mr. Martin!" Jason shot out of the house and down the path. "You're home! It's been boring around here without you."

Gabe snagged the boy before he could barrel into the older man. "Whoa there, Bud. Give Mr. Martin a chance to get in the door, will ya?"

Jason looked up and wrinkled his nose in frustration. "I'll help him. Honest."

Satisfied the boy had calmed down, Gabe released him.

Jason trotted down to the gate and wrapped his arm around the older man like a friend. "Miss Gracie's been cooking, and my mom even made a pie for you."

Martin's face almost glowed. "Um, ham and mashed potatoes?"

"Uh-uh. Grilled chicken and steamed rice. Looks kinda

white, but it smells good. Miss Gracie said the food would be good for you."

Gabe held his breath again, afraid his dad might explode. Though the boy was only the messenger, small details like that had never stopped his dad from shooting.

A rough chuckle filled the air. "Kinda white, huh? Well, maybe we can squirt some ketchup on it and make it look better."

Gabe started up the path again. He shook his head and grinned. Would miracles never cease?

The scent of grilled meat filtered from the kitchen. He stepped inside and dropped the bag to the floor behind the door. Grace stood by the stove, poking at the meat on the indoor grill. Melanie stirred a pot, shaking a spice into the mixture with care. The world had never look more comfortable.

"Hey, Gabriel Thomas," Melanie called from the stove, a dimple creasing in her right cheek as she giggled. "While us women work, how about you set the table?"

He crossed the kitchen, the desire to plant a kiss on her cheek almost unbearable. Instead, he sniffed at the aroma wafting from the pot. "Oh really? Man, you're bossy."

Her eyes grew dark and her grin deepened. The pit of his stomach flipped and he resisted the urge to brush the hair from her eyes. She leaned forward and brushed her nose against his sleeve.

"Ah, much better." She nodded over her shoulder. "Got those dishes?"

Sassy thing. Turning to the stove, he closed his eyes and inhaled. "Mom, what are you cooking?"

Grace gave the chicken one last poke with the stainless-steel tongs before grabbing one and placing it on the platter. "Melanie said her neighbor had a heart attack. She went to classes with her friend and learned to cook so folks could eat."

Gabe sniffed again. "Umm, thanks darlin'."

She shrugged with a grin. “Glad I could help.”

“Smells better in here than anywhere in that hospital.” Martin and Jason crossed the threshold into the kitchen. Jason stepped ahead and pulled out a chair. Martin ruffled the boy’s hair and eased into his place at the table. “I’m starved.”

Gabe grabbed a stack of plates and began passing them around. He drew a deep breath of spices mingled with grilled meat and dish soap. Maybe this healthy eating wasn’t such a bad idea after all.

Melanie wiped her hands and loaded a dish with vegetables. She waved to Jason and handed him the plate. “Careful, it’s hot.”

Jason inched his way back to the table, his concentration centered on the bounty in his hands. He stopped and glanced at Martin. “Mr. Martin, do you like carrots and peas?” At the older man’s nod, Jason continued to the table and laid the food close to Martin.

“Gabe, can you grab the chicken and I’ll get the rice?” Melanie looked up at him with wide blue eyes, a bowl of rice and beans in her hands.

“Absolutely.” As he shuffled around the table with the platter, careful not to bump or spill, the wonder of the meal hit him. His parents, Melanie, Jason, arranging themselves around a table just big enough to fit them all. A space waited for him between his mother and Melanie. He sat down just as Melanie slipped her hand into his on one side, his mother taking his other hand. All the pieces of his life fell together into place.

They bowed their heads for grace, Gabe uttering the familiar words with a new contentment in his heart. At that moment he knew he couldn’t let Melanie and Jason slip away.

Chapter Twelve

Tired from all the excitement of Martin's homecoming the day before, Melanie rejoiced when the meeting of the picnic committee drew to a close.

"Jennifer." She leaned across the table and dug a chart out from under the stack her friend had gathered. "I need this supply list. Unless, of course, *you* want to go shopping for all the decorations."

"No, ma'am. If I'd wanted to oversee this party, I'd have run my own truck off the side of the road." Jennifer grinned. "Pretty sweet deal, if you ask me. Gabe doesn't have to listen to the ladies. All he has to do is replace a few parts."

A few very pricey parts. "This isn't so bad. I kind of like listening to all the squabble. It's friendly enough. Besides, Mrs. Wells gets them to chase around a menu item for a bit and then gives me the final decision." Melanie waved the supply list in the air. "I'm very good at following directions."

Closing her notebook, Jennifer settled the pack in the crook of her arm. She glanced out the window. "Looks like Jason's gotten the hang of the game."

Out back, the boys were playing dodgeball with a soft, red playground ball. Jason dodged a throw. He bounced around to watch the progress of the ball. Another throw came his way. He ducked and ran to the safe line.

"Some games never go out of style, do they?" Melanie stepped out of the kitchen and headed to the playground.

"Thankfully, no." Jennifer closed and locked the door behind her.

"Much better than video games." They stood at the edge of the yard and Melanie waved her arm. "Jason. We have to go."

Jason dodged another throw and came running. "Quick, Mom. Before I get hit." He never stopped moving until he rounded the building and ducked out of sight.

Jennifer tapped her on the shoulder. "C'mon. I'll go with you to the hardware store. I need to pick up some lawn seed anyway."

They drove to Leon's Hardware, where the front display now boasted "Early Summer Sale—Hurry In!" and flats of bedding plants lay stacked around. Shayna sat behind a table looking miserable.

"Hey, Squirt," Jennifer called as they stepped beneath the awning. "You look awful."

"Thanks, Jen." Shayna yawned. "My back muscles hurt and I didn't want to take anything for the pain, so I tossed and turned all night long." She looked at her watch and moaned. "Just noon. What I wouldn't give for a cool room and sleep."

"Why are you out here?" Melanie noticed the pink tinge to Shayna's skin. The lack of breeze didn't help either. "Isn't there something you can do inside?"

"None of the guys want to talk flowers with the women that come in. Besides, Dad is doing inventory, and since I can't lift anything this is really the best place for me."

"Home is the best place for you." Jennifer shook her head. "Just let the customers choose for themselves."

"I can't let my dad down." She put her head on the table

in front of her. "I'm in the shade and sitting down. I can't complain."

Melanie remembered a similar point in her own pregnancy when she would have sold her most prized possession to cuddle down and nap rather than go to the diner and waitress. She had endured winter cold, wet and miserable—a far cry from the hot summer day Shayna fought—but they suffered the same discomfort.

Looked like Shayna needed a friend like that right now, but she'd promised Gabe she'd finish sorting his invoices as soon as the meeting was over. And she had a shed to rummage through for additional decorations. And she'd promised Grace she'd make a heart-healthy dessert for dinner.

When had her time become so scheduled?

Shayna groaned and Jennifer reached out to touch her forehead.

"All you're doing is helping customers select bedding plants?" Melanie glanced over the order sheets on the clipboard on the table. "I can do that for you. Go home and get some rest."

Shayna offered a tired smile. "You can't do that. You don't work here."

"So what? I'll do it as a community service. These are plants, Shayna. This is what I do. Didn't you say your dad owned the hardware store?" She looked to Jennifer for support. "Doesn't she look like she needs to go to bed?"

"Mom, wait." Jason interrupted in a panic. "What am I going to do if you're going to stay and work?"

"I'll take you back to the ranch and you can help around there."

Shayna shook her head. "I can't let you—"

"Jason can spend the afternoon with me." Jennifer patted Jason on the back. "Want to help me sew folks up?"

Jason paled. "Uhhh."

"Only kidding about the sewing. But you could run errands

for me at the hospital. My dad could probably use some help, too." She turned to Shayna, a determined arch to her brow. "I'd say the good Lord just answered your prayer. Go tell your dad you'll see him at home."

Shayna released a long, low sigh. She got up from the table and headed inside. "I love you guys."

Jennifer turned a skeptical eye on Melanie. "Sure this is okay with you?"

Melanie gave Jason a hug and slipped behind the table. "Might as well put that horticulture degree to work. Easier than planning a picnic."

Gabe reached for one of the remaining stakes needed to complete the corral fence. Positioning it beside the fence panel, he swung the hammer and nailed his finger instead of the stake. White-hot pain shot through his hand and up his arm. He dropped the hammer and stuck his hand between his bicep and his ribs.

"Gabe," Jason yelled from the truck that had just driven up. Melanie had called and said she'd be late coming back from town. He'd been casting an eye on the drive all afternoon.

The boy came running up. "Gabe! I got to help Jennifer put on a cast. I handed her tape and gloves and stuff. She said I was a real help."

"I'm sure you were, Bud." Gabe felt his heart pound as Melanie joined them. She looked fine—really more than fine. "You were at the hospital? Everything all right? Shayna okay?"

"She's okay now. Jennifer and I sent her home from the store." She avoided looking at him. "I took over for her."

"Doing what?"

She shook her head. "Answering gardening questions."

"I think I'm missing something. Elwood Leon hired you?" His finger throbbed and he wanted a cool drink. All he was getting was confused. "Can you start at the beginning?"

Jason beamed. “Shayna looked hot. Mom told her to go home. Jennifer took me to the hospital. Mom picked me up. We came home.” He came up for air. “See?”

Gabe lifted a brow at Melanie. “Sure.”

“Gabe.” She drew a deep breath. “Shayna shouldn’t have been out in the hot weather in her condition. I knew something about plants, so I could fill in.”

He studied her. “Is she all right now?”

She nodded and lifted her eyes. “She just needed rest.”

Gabe blew out a breath and winced as his ribs pressed against his finger.

“What’s wrong?” Melanie reached for his wrist and drew out his hand. “What happened?”

“Finger got in the way of the hammer.”

Jason wedged between them. “I know how to fix this, Gabe. Jennifer showed me. Got ice?”

“In the kitchen. Get some ready and I’ll be right in.” Gabe locked on Melanie. “Give me a hand, will you?”

Looking unsure, she nodded. He wrapped his good arm around her shoulders as he held his finger in the air. They started toward the ranch house after Jason took off on a run. “Okay now, tell me what’s wrong.”

They took a couple steps in silence. Then she sighed. “Shayna needed rest and she was worried about letting her dad down. I know I promised to file for you and make dessert for Grace, but I just couldn’t let her sit in the heat like that. Please don’t be angry.”

He stopped, pulling her to a halt beside him. “You thought we’d be mad?”

A small nod answered him. “I’ve got a lot to pay back here.”

Was that all she thought about? Paying him back? His gut twisted. Turning her to face him, Gabe nudged her chin up with his finger until their gazes met. “Sometimes we all get so wrapped up in our own world, it’s hard to think of anyone else.

Mom and I appreciate everything you do for us, especially since Dad's heart attack. But no task is more important than caring about others. Thank you for taking care of Shayna."

Her blue eyes misted. "She was so tired and I know all about plants, and—"

He pulled her into his embrace. "Shayna's lucky to have you as a friend."

She tensed a second and then relaxed. She chuckled into his chest before she lifted her pinkened cheeks. "Am I earning my keep?"

Gabe forgot about the pain in his finger for the lump in his throat. He drew her tight. In a few weeks, memories of a lady with eyes the color of mountain columbines and a smile that stole his breath would be all he'd have left of a summer that changed his life.

He swiped his cheek against her soft hair. "Earning your keep? More than you'll ever know."

"This is dumb. It's Saturday morning, can't I go play?"

Melanie stacked three pine boughs and reached for some ribbon. At the rate she was going, she'd need more than double the amount of supplies she'd collected. "This is not dumb, it's creative. You don't want to just look at food when you sit down to eat."

"Why not?" Jason rolled a pinecone along the tabletop. "If they're hungry."

"Because it's nice having a pretty table, even at a picnic."

"Dumb."

"Hey, anyone home?" Gabe called through the screen door.

"Come in." Melanie finished tying her bow. "We're just putting together centerpieces. How's the finger feeling?"

Gabe flexed his finger at the knuckle. "See? One good night of sleep and I'm a new man."

Jason slumped back into his chair. "Gabe? Do you have to look at something pretty while you eat?"

Gabe leaned against the doorjamb, his arms crossed over his chest. The intensity of his look made her breath catch in her throat. "Don't have to, Bud. But it sure makes everything taste better."

She resisted the urge to pat her hair and straighten her T-shirt. At times, Gabe said the sweetest things that made her long to hear them forever. She shuffled the boughs in front of her.

"Jason, would you please go and collect some more boughs about this size?" She grabbed the cardboard box behind her. "Here. I need about twenty more, and if you see some perfect pinecones throw those in, too."

Jason took the box and squeezed past Gabe. "Is that why cereal tastes better when you look at the box while you eat?"

Gabe chuckled and ruffled Jason's hair. "Something like that, Bud."

The screen door slammed as Jason jumped onto the porch. Gabe removed his hat and took a seat in the empty chair. His presence filled the entire room.

"Pretty tables, huh?" He grinned. "The folks around here never had it so good."

"You've got to be paying me for more than just attending meetings." She stacked another bunch of boughs and measured out the ribbon. "If you hired me as a party planner, that's what you're going to get."

"Just don't go getting too expensive on me. Fixing the dent in your pickup is about all I'm springing for."

She curled the ribbon with her scissors. "If I remember that dollar amount, I'm looking at one pricey fender."

His brows gathered over his sparkling brown eyes, ramping up the wattage of his stare a thousand percent. "I think I'm getting the better end of this deal. So, you still need help?"

Melanie touched a drop of hot glue to a pair of pinecones, setting them in the crook of the boughs. "I told Emma Jean and Frannie I'd have cards for the food."

He scratched his forehead then ran his fingers through his thick, dark hair. Strong, tanned hands rubbed the back of his neck as he stretched. "If you say so."

"Maybe we can find a way to fill all your free time. Want to help cut paper with me?"

The slow, deep grin she earned for that comment made her think twice about voicing blatant observations like that again. She dipped her chin and let her gaze dart over the materials on the table. The breeze no longer blew through the room, and she thought she'd melt.

Reaching out, she rolled a pencil back and forth on the table. "Speaking of labeling dishes, did Mrs. Wells mention anything about adding a main dish to the menu?"

Gabe shook his head, breaking the bond between them. "I don't know how you did it, but I've got a hundred pounds of pork ribs coming in this week. Sweetheart, you're making history."

Her heart jumped at the endearment, even if it was only an expression. "You won't be sorry. My uncle used to season the best ribs. I know the grocery store has the spices. The trick is in the rubbing."

"I'll be sure to take notes."

"Gabe, you've got to broaden your horizons."

"You're managing that quite well." He pushed back from the table, the legs of the chair scraping on the wooden floor. "So, are you planning on flipping all those ribs?"

"Nope, RJ is going to help me. And Hank said he'd take the grills with the beef. See? All bases covered."

Gabe leaned back in the chair, his jaw jutted out. "And who is going to help me with the cattle?"

Excited to share all her plans, Melanie set aside the pencil and waved her finger in a circle. "It all comes around. Most of your setup occurs now. On Saturday, Hank and RJ will get the fires going and begin the meat. Mrs. Wells volunteered her husband and a couple others to take over when you need Hank and RJ for the auction. All they have to do is fill platters and serve." She flipped her hands over, palms up. "Everything is falling into place. You were right. The ladies of Hawk Ridge know how to organize an event."

"I don't remember offering my men to help."

She wasn't going to let him rain on her schedule. This picnic was coming together better than she'd ever dreamed. Better than she thought she could do. "Gabe, trust me."

"Is that right?" Gabe challenged, his dark eyes unwavering.

Her cheeks flamed under his scrutiny. She should have never opened her mouth. "Careful you don't get blisters on your fingers from the scissors."

Boots pounded up the path and onto the porch. RJ rattled the screen door. "Hey, Gabe. Miss Grace wants you back at the house. Shipment of cattle coming our way."

Gabe pinched the bridge of his nose and squeezed his eyelids closed. "I'll be glad when this auction is over." He opened his eyes and scrubbed his hand down his face.

An odd disappointment settled in her belly. "Jason can come back and help me."

"This won't take me long." Gabe stood up and settled his hat on his head. He reached the doorway. "No sense in tearing the boy away from a day collecting pine droppings."

The crooked grin on his face filled Melanie with hope. Maybe they'd still get to work together today. She didn't have much time left to spend at the Circle D, and she wanted to make the most of it. A long-forgotten hint of sass tickled her tongue. "I've seen RJ heft bales of hay. I'll bet he can help me cut all the cards I need."

"I think you've penciled in enough Hank-and-RJ time into your schedule. I'll be back." His rich brown eyes held her gaze. He broke the spell with a tap of his finger on her nose. "Unloading cattle will just be a warm-up for all that scissor cutting."

Gabe pushed through the screen door and headed down the dirt path. He ran his fingers through his hair before setting his hat in place, never missing a step. Melanie watched his fluid movements until he rounded the corner and moved out of sight.

She looked down at the pile of greenery on the table in front of her and felt a giddy smile tug at her lips. She'd better start thinking of lots of dishes to label.

Chapter Thirteen

"Hurry, Jason, we're going to make everyone late." Melanie dabbed on the last touch of mascara. Checked her lip gloss and blush, too. "I don't think Gabe wants to be late for church."

Jason stepped into her doorway. "I'm ready, Mom. Are you? Hey, you look good."

Good? Jeans, a long-sleeved shirt and hiking boots. Thankfully, everything clean. She gave Jason the once-over. "Hmm, you do, too. Amazing what a little soap and water will do." She pointed him toward the door and they both took off at a run.

Gabe and Hank sat at the bottom of their path in the same shiny, clean SUV they'd ridden in last Sunday. Melanie slowed to a walk, hiding a grin. The truck was dressed up for church, too. Gabe got out and opened the door for them. Jason climbed in the back, where Hank had already switched seats.

"Hank, don't you want to ride shotgun?" She peered in the back window.

"Not on Sunday, ma'am." He tousled Jason's hair. "Can't let Jason here get bored on the ride into town."

Gabe rolled his eyes. "Don't mind him. He just beat me to gallant. Mom's staying home with Dad today. Dad's madder than a hornet about it." He opened her door and let her get settled before closing it. Rounding the front of the vehicle, he slid into his seat, dropped into gear and away they drove. "We all have to pray our hardest for patience. For us, and him."

Not ten minutes later, they pulled into the church parking lot. Before Gabe could get out of the car, people surrounded him asking about Martin. Gabe assured them his dad was okay, just resting this morning.

They followed him like a swarm of bees as he skirted the front of the truck and opened her door to let her out. Cupping her shoulder, he guided her across the yard. The heat of his palm penetrated her cotton shirt as she greeted the people she'd met over the week. They talked to her, surrounded her.

RJ met them at the door, his dark hair still damp and his shirt pressed. He grinned and nodded. Melanie responded, marveling over all the friendships she'd forged in such a short time. How was she going to leave?

She followed Gabe to the same pew they'd sat in last Sunday. She didn't mind sitting up front as much as she had the previous week. Outside the plate-glass window behind the pulpit, the sun brightened the peaks, casting crazy shadows along the jagged edges. Green grasses grew in the short field beyond the church, their tips a good three inches high. She'd ask Gabe about loading the tractor and mower and giving the grass a trim. Wouldn't take long at all.

The processional music stopped and the pastor entered, wishing everyone a good morning. Melanie relaxed even further as the kind man smiled at the congregation and reviewed the activities in the week ahead. He asked the congregation to keep Martin in their prayers. He also must have had some insight into the storms brewing at home, because he asked everyone to pray for Grace and the rest of the family, too, in this time of uncertain patience. He looked over at Gabe and nodded.

Gabe stood from his seat beside her and walked up to the

front where guitars and a keyboard stood. The pew felt empty without him. Melanie wrapped her arms around her waist.

Hank stood and joined him. So did Jennifer. And Ruthy and Janet, the young women from the planning meeting the other morning. Gabe grabbed the guitar and looped the strap into place.

"Being the last Sunday of the month, let's tell the Lord how we really feel about the blessings He's given us." Gabe strummed a couple chords, and everyone rose. Music filled the room. The congregation sang.

Melanie stared in amazement at the front of the sanctuary. Gabe played guitar as if he'd been a musician his entire life. Eyes closed during the verse, he sang with his heart in every word. At the refrain, he opened his eyes, his fingers dancing on the strings, the power of his music incredible. By the end of the first song, Melanie realized she sang with just as much gusto as everyone else. She loved it.

The band played two more songs, each speaking a different message to her heart. The years melted away, and Melanie felt as if she'd never left the church, never suffered anguish, never doubted God's wisdom.

She almost cried.

As the last chords were strummed, her heart splintered and all the fight in her washed away. Jason bumped into her as his voice quieted at the end of the song. She reached out and hugged him until he squirmed.

She'd been wrong to keep Jason from the fellowship of believers due to her own bitter feelings. She'd accepted the consequences of her actions, and God had been faithful in His care of them. She loved Jason with her whole heart and wouldn't have wanted her course to go any other way. She offered thanks to the Lord for His wisdom and mercy.

The band finished and returned to their seats. Gabe slid in beside Melanie. Love and adoration for the Lord shone in Gabe. Not just in church but in everything the man did. She'd thank him later for opening her eyes to the truth of living God's love.

After church, the ladies of the picnic committee surrounded her. Jason squirmed away, saying he'd be at the swing. Melanie wished she could be there, too.

"The Davidson place looks wonderful with everything spruced up for the picnic." Mrs. Wells clapped her hands together. "Gracie's pleased as punch that the fences have been washed down and the equipment moved out of her view. And she never thought she'd see the day when Gabe took notice of a lovely lady over his cows."

"Heard tell he took an afternoon off to go fishing." Frannie Pollard nodded at the group.

Emma Jean looked around wide-eyed. "Came by the church the other day to play on the swing, too."

Melanie searched the expectant faces for some hint of a joke. She wanted to laugh at the curiosity she found. The church ladies of Hawk Ridge read far too much into simple courtesies. "I'm much more a bother to the entire Davidson family than you think. My truck needed repairs and I needed a place to stay. I'm just paying the family back for their hospitality by helping with the picnic."

Mrs. Bingham took Melanie's hand and patted her knuckles. "That Gabriel is not torn off task easily. I do believe you've caught the young man's eye." Gnarled fingers stilled on Melanie's hand as Mrs. Bingham moved closer. "All of Gracie's boys are nice, but that Gabriel, he's my favorite."

Melanie offered a skeptical smile even as thousands of butterflies fluttered in her stomach. For as much as the thought of Gabe showing interest excited her, reality told her love didn't happen this way. Other predicaments, yes; love, no. "I think Grace raised him a gentleman. Like I said, he's just stuck with me until my truck is fixed."

"If you say so, my dear." Mary Wells tipped her chin and pinned Melanie with a challenging look right over the top of her wire-rimmed glasses. "And you will be with us for how long?"

"The picnic is next Saturday and I'll be leaving on Sunday. I have to get back to Colorado Springs. My vacation will be over."

Emma Jean, Frannie, all of the ladies, nodded with Mary Wells.

"Pam is getting buckets of potato salad ready. Missy and Cara are collecting desserts." Mrs. Bingham focused back on the picnic. She released Melanie's hand in favor of pointing in the direction of the kitchen. "Ruthy has everyone coming at eleven o'clock. Is that all right?"

"The meat will be done and so will the beans. I looked around for the best places to put the tables and everything fit." Melanie eyed the group but saw nothing more than business at hand. "I'm praying like a madwoman we don't have rain."

"You and all the folks in the county. If God sends rain, then He has a good reason to do it. Oh, and we'll be praying for you, too." Mrs. Wells winked at Melanie. "For everything to work out."

Shop talk settled over the women, each excited about the food, the fun and the fellowship of the upcoming Saturday. Melanie chatted with them, her heart filled with incredible tenderness for the kind people of Hawk Ridge. They'd treated her and Jason as if they belonged from the very first day. Peace settled over her, a peace she hadn't embraced in years.

Gabe's deep laughter floated over the noise and caught her attention. He stood with RJ, Jennifer and a couple of men by the parking lot. Joy touched every line of his face as he nodded over something one of the men said. She had to agree with her church ladies. God had made a special man in Gabe Davidson.

A flash of longing stabbed Melanie's contentment. As soon as the picnic was over and her truck repaired, she'd return to the city, to her old life, and pick up the search for a job again.

After spending time in Hawk Ridge, she knew she wanted life in a small town. Maybe she'd even find another community much like Hawk Ridge, one with the perfect job just for her. But she'd never find another man like Gabe. Or the friends she'd made. The friends she'd miss. Gabe belonged to this community. They each had their own special places that didn't include the other.

She'd coordinated the barbecue as agreed. Her filing and sorting in Gabe's office had begun. Her truck received resuscitation with a repaired radiator and carb.

Agreement signed, sealed and delivered.

Gabe's laughter floated over her again.

Somehow, the thought of leaving Hawk Ridge didn't thrill her as much as it had a couple of weeks earlier.

"King Phillip Came Over From Great Spain…"

Gabe turned at the sound of Melanie's voice in the corner of his office. With the second drawer of his vertical file opened to the fullest, she sat on the edge of his desk scribbling on a pad of paper.

"No wait, that's not right. How about For Great Spaghetti?" She tapped the tip of her pencil on the pad. "Good Soup? Nope."

"What are you mumbling about?" He stepped into the room. Organized stacks of manila file folders lined the front edge of his desk where only days ago a scattered mess of paper lay.

He could get used to this.

A smile tugged at her lips. "It's Great Spain. I had that botany class right before lunch. I know I would have thought of nothing but food if soup or spaghetti were involved."

"In what?"

"Plant family classifications."

What was he missing? "Plant classification for…?" He curled his fingers as if to pull the information out of her.

"For organization. In botany class I used a mnemonic to remember my plant family classification. You know—*K*ing *P*hillip *C*ame *O*ver and so on, to remember *K*ingdom, *P*hyllum, *C*lass..." She fanned her fingers and rolled her wrist to indicate her continuing pattern. She pointed to his file cabinet. "You need a system or you're going to start piling papers all over the place again. Not efficient at all."

"But I knew where everything was. Now I'll have to dig around in the *organized* files to find what I need."

She held up a crumpled pink sheet of paper and waved it at him. "Really? Do you know what this is?"

"I'm sure you're going to tell me."

"This is a receipt for hydraulic oil. From two years ago. Nine hundred ninety-one dollars. Don't you need stuff like this for taxes?"

Bookkeeping had never been his forte. No wonder Zac kept pestering him about his quarterly reports. How much else did he leave off the cash flow accounting?

Melanie continued to stare at him, the crinkles around her eyes totally blowing her stern facade. He gave her a quick shrug. "Hmm, well, what do you know?"

She scrunched her nose at him before turning back to the file drawer, her ponytail swinging with indignation. "I know enough *not* to leave tax prep in your capable hands."

A quick shot of heat hit him like an archery arrow on its mark. Capable? She thought him capable? He liked the sounds of that.

She flipped through the hanging files. Sliding the folder into place, Melanie nodded her head, and a dimple appeared in her cheek as she waved her hand over the drawer. "See?"

He saw, all right. Now he needed to quit staring. "I love it when you talk scientific to me."

Her grin widened and she pushed her firm palm into his chest. "Don't mess with me, cowboy. I can twist your system into knots just as easy as I've untangled it."

He didn't doubt it at all. Just look at what her simple banter did to his insides. If he didn't tamp down his hyped-up awareness of her, he'd be worthless to the entire Circle D operation. "So how about taking the afternoon off? The carnival's in town."

She pushed against the file drawer until it slid into place. "Carnival, huh? Rides and games?"

"Popcorn, peanuts and candied apples, too." He hiked a thigh along the edge of his desk. "Today's the last day. They leave tomorrow."

"Hmm, I haven't been to a carnival in years." She raised her brow, giving him another of her challenging looks. "I suppose Jason is excited to go."

"I wouldn't know, ma'am. I thought I'd come clear it with the boss first. This ol' cowboy learns his lessons fast."

Her dimple reappeared. "Good thing. You wouldn't know where my son is, would you?"

Gabe scooped up a pile of receipts and tapped them into a straight pile. "Down in the corral helping Hank. Actually, now that I think about it, Jason sits on his horse and *looks* like he's helping Hank."

She nodded. "That's my boy. I suppose you like all the wild rides."

"No, ma'am." His stomach fluttered like the spray of a deck of cards having nothing to do with the thought of rides, wild or tame. He cleared his throat and grappled for composure. "I'm more a merry-go-round kinda guy, myself."

Not an hour later, Melanie strolled the sidewalks of Hawk Ridge with Gabe and Hank. Jason ran in front of them. People said hi in passing. They stopped and chatted with folks who told her the advice she'd given them at Leon's Hardware made a world of difference with their gardens, flowers and lawns. Giddiness bubbled inside of her. She never dreamed sharing her horticulture knowledge would garner so much excitement from the crowd.

Obviously, she underestimated how the town viewed their landscaping.

Small shops lined the quaint main street with brick-paved sidewalks, all doors open in the summer weather. Although the shops normally remained closed on Sunday, today the shopkeepers made an exception. The carnival brought everyone to town.

"Look, Mom, a candy shop."

That was all the warning Jason gave before he ducked into a doorway with sweet fragrances of caramel popcorn wafting out. Melanie followed, the smell too good to be true. Black-and-white floor tiles edged up to a soda counter complete with old-fashioned rotating pedestal seats. Display cases lined the opposite side of the store. A few shoppers studied the goodies and pointed at jellied candies and plates of chocolate truffles.

"Want a malt? Ed Bergin makes the best strawberry malts in the world." Gabe rested his thigh on a stool as he leaned against the counter. "How about it, Bud? Think you can finish one of Ed's specials?"

"You bet." Jason climbed up on the seat beside Gabe. "Can I, Mom?"

How could she say no? "Only if you promise to share with the rest of us."

Jason followed Ed's every move as he grabbed a silver malt container, heaped in ingredients and flicked the switch to the blender.

"Hey, Ed, better make that three of those. Hank and I promise to share, too."

Now it was Melanie's eyes that grew wide. "You're kidding! Look at the size of those canisters."

Ed turned off the machine and lifted the silver container

from the base. He poured out the contents into a glass at least a foot tall.

"Here you go, young man." He slipped the drink in front of Jason. "You'll never taste a better malted than this."

The straw stuck straight up in the thick mixture. Jason kneeled on his seat and brought the straw to his mouth. One long draw later, he grinned from ear to ear. "Yes, sir, Mr. Bergin. The best ever."

Ed tweaked Jason's nose. "That's what I love to hear. You let me know if you need a refill, ya hear?"

Ed mixed up a couple more. Gabe paid and slid one to Hank before sticking a couple of straws in his own. "You go first." He offered Melanie the glass. "Best ever."

Gabe remained propped against the stool. Melanie stepped up to the counter and brought the straw to her lips. Flavors of tart, sweet strawberries and thick cream slid down her throat. In all her years of drinking shakes and malts, she'd never tasted anything like it. "Mmm, best ever."

Gabe dipped his head and took a drink from his straw. They stood nose to nose as she looked into his gold-flecked eyes and suddenly the notion of sharing a drink became very intimate. She drew the straw from her mouth and licked her lips to catch the last of the strawberry flavor. Dimples appeared in his cheeks as Gabe drew the thick drink up his straw. He winked at her as he straightened and swallowed.

A crazy zing of awareness zipped down her back. She swayed toward him, her hair brushing his cheek. Gabe stilled beside her and she became aware she'd stalled at his shoulder. She moved aside without meeting his gaze, her stomach a knot of nervous energy. If she'd moved just a hair closer, she might not have been able to move away.

Get a grip.

The lazy spin of overhead ceiling fans hummed in the air. She turned toward the display case next to her and pretended interest in the dark chocolate truffles.

"Now what do you think about that?" Melanie pointed at the yellow, orange and green candy shaped like fruit slices. "Old-fashioned jellied fruit. I haven't tasted those in years."

Ed Bergin pulled out the tray and let her choose the slices she wanted. Rich, dark chocolate truffles too, but she couldn't put the strawberry malt out of her mind.

"Ed, while you're at it, bag up a pound of taffy, okay?" Gabe rested his elbow on the glass top. "Jason doesn't have any loose teeth, does he?"

"No." She studied the truffles before her as if their shape and texture might appear on a final exam someday. "Nothing loose at the moment."

"Good. Ed? Make that two pounds." He waved his finger at the confections in front of her. "And an assortment of your finest."

She looked up. "They look delicious."

"They are." Gabe nodded at the choices Ed made. "But once you've tasted the taffy, all else will pale."

I doubt it. Nothing would wipe away the memory of that strawberry malt.

Bagged candy in hand, the crew hit the streets again. Gabe dug out a piece of taffy, unwrapped it and offered it to Melanie. She opened her mouth and he popped it in. Soft and chewy, the taffy refused to break down. She worked it through her mouth and only managed to stick her teeth together.

"Mom," Jason called through clenched teeth. "It won't let go."

Watching the concentration on the little boy's face, Melanie laughed. Where was a camera when you needed one? Gabe chuckled beside her.

"Okay gang, think of the taffy as quicksand." Gabe held his hands out as if to calm the waters. "The more you fight it, the more it holds firm. Just relax your jaw and the sugar will release from your teeth."

As the taffy came loose, Melanie balled the mound into

her cheek. Slow melt worked much better. The whole lot of them must have looked crazy standing on the sidewalk, jaws glued shut and laughing like there was no tomorrow.

Tomorrow. She'd begun to dread the coming of the days.

"C'mon, Bud. Let's go see what kind of arm you have." Gabe pointed toward the midway.

Melanie fell in line behind them as they slipped between booths until he found the one he was looking for. Three bottles, stacked two on the bottom and one on top, sat at the back of the booth. The handler gave Jason three balls. All it took was one strike for all three to fall and he'd win the prize of his choice.

"Bud, now study the setup. You want to hit the bottle on the bottom, the one on the left side, because it's holding up more of the top bottle, okay?"

"Okay." Jason concentrated and threw. The ball flew way off to the left. Gabe caught her gaze, his golden-brown eyes sparkling. He hunched over with an exaggerated wince. Feathers tickled her insides again. A shaky smile crossed her lips when Jason wound up for another throw.

Lots of patience and many tokens later, bells and whistles went off in the booth, signaling a happy winner. Gabe gave Jason a hug and whispered something in his ear. Jason nodded and pointed at a stuffed yellow dog in the back row. The handler poked it with a long pole and brought it down. Grabbing the prize with both arms, Jason came running.

"Look, Mom!" His toothy grin overcame his face. "Look what I won for you!"

"For me?" The stuffed toy stood almost as tall as her son. "But honey, *you* won him."

"Yep." His grin grew wider. "But the first prize of the evening always goes to the prettiest girl."

Heat scorched across her cheeks. *The prettiest girl.* She glanced at Gabe. He shrugged, and nodded at Jason.

An older couple stopped and patted her shoulder. "Your young man has fine manners."

"Thank you." Which young man they meant, she wasn't sure. And she didn't care. She bent down and hugged Jason, burying her nose in his bony shoulder. "Honey, it's the most wonderful present I've ever received."

He hugged her back and then stuffed the dog in her arms. "Hank, look what I won!" His eyes opened wider. "Hey, Jennifer!"

Ever since Jennifer had convinced Melanie to try the swing, the sun rose and set on her in Jason's eyes. She waved as she caught sight of them.

"Hi everyone." Jennifer pushed her sleeves up her arms as she stopped beside them. "I thought I'd never find you in this crowd."

"Look what I won for Mom." Jason patted the bottom half of the dog. "You always give the prize to the prettiest girl."

"Wow, your mom is the luckiest."

Jason displayed his muscles. "Now I better win a prize for you since I'm going to be a doctor when I grow up."

"Oh you are, are you?" Jennifer placed her hands on her hips. "Why would you want to do that?"

"So I can wear a cool coat and play around with scissors and bandages all day like you do."

"Okay, Bud." Hank stepped up as Jennifer's mouth fell open and directed Jason to another booth. "How about we try our luck with darts?"

Chapter Fourteen

Gabe was the luckiest guy at the carnival.

As they wandered through the rows of vendors, he listened to Jennifer gab about different foods, fun games and the crowded midway. She seemed full of words that couldn't help spill out. Melanie held tight to the stuffed dog and gabbed back with equal enthusiasm. People smiled at them as they passed, and he knew it sure wasn't because of him.

Gabe had never experienced having a beautiful woman on each arm until tonight.

Of course, technically, they weren't on each arm. No way was he going to get in the middle of their feminine nattering. He escorted them, perfectly content to have Melanie beside him with her attention directed toward Jennifer.

The sun had dipped behind the peaks a little while earlier, and the lights of the rides and midway were turning up as the sunlight turned down. Kids ran all around them. Teenage boys walked awkwardly beside teenage girls who dragged them from game to game, ride to ride. Hawkers dipped into the crowd looking for players. Gabe grinned, remembering the thrill the carnival always brought to town.

"What do you think, Gabe?" Jen looked at him.

"About what?" He turned to the two expectant faces.

She rolled her eyes. "Riding the Ferris wheel. Let's climb on before it gets pitch-black over the valley."

Mountain peak shadows lengthened as the sun sank lower. "Sure. Looks better when we can see beyond the ring of lights. How many tokens?"

Melanie shifted the dog in her hands. She bounced on her toes like a little kid. Fidgeting with the toy, she tilted her head toward the bench seats swaying with the wheel.

"Don't worry, the dog will fit on the seat with us."

She beamed. "Have you seen Jason?"

Jennifer looked around the crowd, her keen eyes checking out all the lines. "There's Hank. I'm sure Jason's not too far behind." Her face brightened. "Oh, look. There's RJ." She tugged on Melanie's sleeve. "Now there's a cowboy for you. Maybe he wants to ride with us. RJ!"

Melanie dug her hand into her pocket and pulled out a handful of tokens. Wisps of blond hair fell across her cheek as she watched Jen wave RJ over. Gabe reached out and tucked the hair behind her ear, the strands as soft as down. She graced him with a smile that lit up his world as she shifted the dog square in front of her.

"I know I have more tokens." She handed the golden disks to him. "I held some back so Jason wouldn't spend them all in one place."

His palm heated as her fingers remained locked with his. Packs of teenagers moved between rides like misplaced amoebas. Couples, young and old, strolled the midway. And Gabe didn't want to let go, not for all the tokens in the world.

Her fingers slipped away as Jason ran up. "I won a stuffed pig for Jennifer. Told her it would make her remember the barbecue." Bouncing as if springs loaded his shoes, Jason pointed across the lot. "Look, a Tilt-a-Whirl. Wanna ride with me?"

"You bet." Melanie grabbed his hand as if he might take off without her. She turned and offered Gabe her dog. "Will you hold this? You never know what gravity will do to people in one of those things."

He accepted the stuffed animal. Melanie captured his hand and pulled him with them. Pink and blue cotton candy on paper tubes bobbed up and down in the hands of excited kids, and the scent of fried funnel cakes filled the air. At the ride line, Melanie pulled Gabe and Jason together like window draperies.

She peeked between them. "Jennifer and RJ an item?"

Gabe twisted around. RJ stood with Jen in line for the Ferris wheel. Jen gabbed with her usual animation and RJ appeared enthralled. "If they were, it would be news for the whole town."

"Every tidbit is news for this town."

But Jennifer and RJ would make the front page. "Yeah, well."

Hank strolled up and stood on the other side of Jen. The line moved and all three of them squeezed into a seat. "I think she's well chaperoned."

Melanie still held his hand. Her fingers squeezed. The small gesture tickled his insides. He squeezed back and looked up at the top of the ride as it squealed to a halt. "Don't suppose I can talk you into that merry-go-round ride, huh?"

"You weren't kidding, were you?" A smile he couldn't decipher danced on her lips. "That's okay. Thanks for holding the dog."

She gave his fingers a final squeeze before she followed Jason through the line into the monstrous contraption.

His fingers tingled and his palm felt empty without her hand.

Lights flashed and music blared as the ride began to spin. Colors blurred until the entire wheel looked like it could shoot off into space. His stomach turned even though he stood on solid ground. Minutes later, the ride slowed and stopped. Gabe braced, ready to help Melanie no matter her condition.

She walked toward him, her cheeks flushed. "That is the most amazing ride."

Amazing was right. She didn't look a bit fazed.

"Jason. How was it?" A frown replaced her delight.

He held on to his mother's arm, his skin pasty and cheeks drawn.

"Hey Bud, looks like the wind kinda blew out of your sails." Gabe packed the dog beneath his arm. He reached over with his other hand and urged the boy toward him. "Let's go for a walk. I'll bet you'll feel better once you get your land legs back." He started to reposition the dog when his gaze collided with the deepest, bluest, most troubled eyes he'd ever seen. Eyes that pleaded with him. For what, he wasn't sure. "Melanie. You okay?"

"Yeah, stomach like a rock." She clasped her arms across her chest. "I should have known better. After all he's eaten today. Putting him into a musical centrifuge wasn't a good idea."

Rethinking his strategy, Gabe handed the stuffed canine to her and steered Jason toward the parking lot. He looked over his shoulder and hoped his grin encouraged her. "Go find Hank. I think someone's fun meter just maxed out."

"Everyone comfortable back there?" Hank gripped the wheel of the SUV and swung onto the main road out of town.

"Perfect." Gabe answered in hushed tones beside her. "Just take it easy on the curves, okay?"

Melanie stroked Jason's hair back from his forehead, as he lay across her lap, asleep. Way too much fun today. Malteds, cotton candy, hot dogs and taffy, all swirled together by a Tilt-a-Whirl, did not a good combination make.

Gabe handled it like a real trooper.

"Hank, you're doing fine." She touched Jason's cheek, relieved to find it cool. "Thanks for driving. I like the way

Gabe thinks when there's disaster a-brewing. Good thing to have him back here, just in case."

"Yes, ma'am," Hank chuckled, his grin spread wide in the reflection of the rearview mirror. "Good thing for the boss to handle."

"Glad I could help, ma'am." Gabe settled back. The cushion of the seat dipped under his weight and she leaned with the shift.

His voice rumbled in his chest as he and Hank spoke of people he'd seen. Wedged between Gabe on one side, his arm stretched across the back of the seat, and Jason snuggled beside her on the other, Melanie burrowed into her little hollow and relaxed. Heat emanated through his cotton shirt and chased away the chill in the night air.

From the moment she'd seen the Ferris wheel, she knew she wanted to ride it. With Gabe. Strange flutters flew through her body as she thought how close she'd come to touching the icy white stars in the midnight black sky on a ride whirling through the cool air.

Sitting beside Gabe.

She indulged in a fantasy she hadn't considered in years. A fantasy she yearned to fulfill if the past didn't keep getting in the way. A past she didn't think Gabe and his family would approve of any more than had her own.

Jason snuggled into her lap and peace filled her. She fingered his cotton T-shirt, remembering his toddler years. Wild assortments of food tossed in his belly at the same time didn't sit well with him back then, either. She rubbed her back against Gabe and settled deeper into the seat cushion. She thought about the taffy…and the stuffed dog…and the taste of Gabe's malt….

And then she didn't think about anything except calloused fingers brushing her hair.

"Hey, Bud, you ready to go?"

Gabe's voice boomed into the little cabin through the open

door. Melanie shot out of her bedroom, one shoe on, one shoe off. After last night, she couldn't image Jason wanting to ride anything. "He ran down to the house. Where are you going?"

"Town." Gabe opened the screen and stepped inside the kitchen.

Crisp blue jeans, a cotton shirt and his black hat all looked great on the man. Melanie fought the urge to touch the spot on the top of her head where he'd run his fingers through her hair as she'd slept. Her cheeks warmed. Best nap she'd had in years.

She blew the thoughts out of her mind as she dropped her other shoe and stuck her foot in it. "Leave something behind last night?"

His eyes sparkled as a slow grin spread across his face. "Mom shoved a list in my hand and told me not to take too long. Thought I'd take Bud with me, since Hank and the boys are moving cattle in the south fields, Dad has a headache and Mom said you were helping her in the kitchen this morning."

"Gabe." She shook her head. "You don't have to babysit."

"Babysit?" His eyes grew wide. "Bud's my bud. We've got guy shopping to do." He leaned toward her. The same scent as the evening before brought back memories of a solid chest she'd commandeered as a pillow. She dipped toward him and their shoulders bumped. Melanie pressed firm.

His breath tickled her ear. "Besides, I want to get him something, if that's okay with you. Something to remember us by."

As if Jason would ever forget the weeks he spent on the Davidson ranch. As if *she* ever would. Gabe Davidson was the most thoughtful man she'd ever met. At times like this, she wished her life had been different. But then, if it had, she probably never would have met Gabe in the first place. "Don't spoil him too badly."

His lingering gaze stole all rational thought. "No, ma'am."

He ducked out the door. Melanie watched him amble down her path back to the ranch house, his steps sure and solid. She swallowed the lump in her throat. Grabbing her sweat jacket, she pushed past the screen door. Maybe she needed more to remember him by, too. "I'll walk down to the house with you."

She fell into step as they followed the path through the trees. They passed a tributary path leading to another cabin tucked in the trees.

"You said you normally have these cabins full in the summer. I'll bet the help love having their families close by." She pushed a bushy pine bough out of her way.

"The guys stay up here all summer from all parts of Colorado, Wyoming and Montana. Their families come visit when they can. Everyone is so busy with ball practices, swimming lessons, work, we hardly ever have anyone here in one cabin all summer."

"But this year you only have RJ?"

"Manny lives in town. His cousins Gus and Raul work here during the summer. We hire as we need. Too many idle men make for trouble."

"So the guys up here have families?"

"Hank is family." Gabe grinned as if proud of his own wit.

Melanie elbowed him in the ribs.

"And RJ?" Memories of Jennifer hanging on RJ's every word the night before flashed through her mind.

"Nick sent him with the cattle knowing we were short on help this summer. He's a good worker, with strong, ethical values." Gabe swiped at a swarm of gnats clouded around them. "I'm hoping he stays."

She nodded, relieved. "Glad you invite families to visit."

"Seems to make the most sense. Getting to Hawk Ridge from anywhere takes hours, and the work goes all summer long. The guys get days off, but no guarantee it's Saturday and Sunday, or even if the days are together. Depends on what they're good at and how much and when we need them."

"What kind of time do you take off?"

"When you run your own business, the boss is always the last to turn the lights off."

"You seem to have time for us."

"I don't want to tell you what time I turn *my* lights off."

Many nights she knew he left his office well past her bedtime. "That late?"

He shrugged. "Ranching by day, paperwork by night."

"I thought you had help. The office is in your parents' house."

"The office has always been there, so why mess with a good thing? And besides, it gives me a chance to finish up shop. When I walk over to my place, I leave the work behind. It's a mental thing."

"If you keep up this pace, you probably *will* go mental. Glad I was able to straighten up and file for you." Pride filled her at the difference in the office space since she'd spent a few hours organizing. "Call me when things get out of hand again."

"Promise you'll come?"

She glanced up at him, impossible to study his face as they moved. He took two more steps then stopped and turned toward her, giving her the advantage of standing higher on the path so they were almost face-to-face. He tipped his hat back and let the morning sunshine bathe his face in light.

Melanie searched for dark circles under his eyes or evidence of strain around his lips. Instead, all she saw was a firm jawline, a straight nose and well-drawn lips that twitched under her scrutiny. A tiny dimple appeared at the corner of his mouth.

She was a goner for his crooked smile.

Insects buzzed around in the summer sun. The natter of

ground squirrels blended with the whistles of the jays. His shallow breaths warmed her cheeks.

He stood before her, watching her. Waiting for her answer.

She remembered his gentle touch atop her head as she'd dozed against him the night before. She so wanted to touch her lips to his, to know safety and trust.

He cleared his throat. "Well?"

In his dark eyes, she read a longing that matched her own. The air stilled around them as he drew closer and touched his lips to hers.

Nothing prepared her for the tenderness that passed between them. His palm cradled her cheek and she didn't know whether to rub against the rough skin or move closer to deepen the kiss. In the end, she didn't have to choose. Gabe drew back, his dark eyes locked on hers while his fingers wove through her hair.

A soft breeze carried strands of hair across her face.

"I'm sorry, I should've asked first." Gabe ran his finger down her cheek before dropping his hand. "I've wanted to do that for a while."

"I—" Melanie licked her lips and swallowed, grappling for words. "I don't want to complicate matters."

She drew a breath as he studied her, searching for something she hoped she had the right answer for.

As if coming to a decision, he offered her a gentle smile. "I promise not to tell."

He stepped to the side and allowed her to continue down the trail. Her mind revved at a billion rpm. They only had a few more days to spend here in paradise. She had to go back to her real world. One without cowboys. And barbecues. And pregnant young ladies loved and encouraged by the entire town.

She'd only been here a couple weeks. How could she become so attached? Melanie stole a glance and found him staring at her. Her face warmed and she couldn't keep from smiling.

"I've wanted to kiss you for a long time, too."

His dimple deepened and he looked ahead. "I'm glad."

They crossed the parking area without saying a word. Gabe opened the gate and she darted into the yard. Voices filtered out of the kitchen door.

"Well, it's about time you got down here." Grace set a couple of bowls on the table. "We're baking pies this morning."

Gabe leaned against the doorjamb, his casual stance igniting every nerve in her body. Melanie knew if she remained by his side she'd most likely disgrace herself and her family by saying something stupid. Or worse.

Baskets of berries sat on the counter. She angled around the table and peered into the fruit. "Pies sound great."

Grace set down a flour canister and measuring cups as Melanie grabbed a seat at the table. She ventured a look at Gabe. His grin made her face heat.

"Going to town sometime today, Gabriel?" Grace pulled out a chair for herself and sat down.

"Hmm." Gabe pushed away from the wall. "Make sure you make a pie for tastin', too."

Grace nodded. "Of course. Now get going and bring back the supplies."

Gabe tipped his hat and added a long, slow stare for Melanie.

She thought she would melt.

Chapter Fifteen

"Honestly, that boy is a smart one when it comes to ranching, but he gets a little thick when he's preoccupied."

Melanie grabbed one of the mugs of coffee on the table and took a drink. "The barbecue is only a week away and he's still receiving cattle and bulls for the auction. I guess he has reason."

The older woman lifted her gray eyes and held Melanie's gaze with gentleness and understanding. "The good Lord knew what He was doing when He sent you to us. I just want to return the favor and help you however we can."

"I'm not looking for anything in return." Melanie picked a berry out of the bowl. "I'm planning Gabe's party and he's fixing my truck. Your hospitality already goes far beyond anything I've dreamed."

She nibbled at the edges before popping the treat in her mouth. "I haven't ridden a horse in years, Grace. Sure feels good to know I still can sit a saddle. Jason's been having the time of his life up here. It's going to be hard going back home after the great few weeks he's had being a cowboy."

"Well, give him a whole summer of fun then. You don't have to rush back for anything, do you?"

"Only back to my sole means of support until I can find

a job that appreciates the intricacies of mothering. I'm not going to stop looking. If I found this last one, I know there are others."

"What about sending Jason to spend time with your parents? Kids grow up fast. Be a shame if they miss everything."

"Grace, I appreciate your interest, but really, this isn't a good idea."

"Could you be any worse off if you tried?"

A lump lodged in Melanie's throat. She didn't want to talk about this… She looked away and shook her head.

The chair slid across the wooden floor and Grace stepped up beside her, resting her hand on Melanie's shoulder. "We parents, we do all we can. God repairs our mistakes if we let Him."

Grace gave a quick squeeze before moving to the counter, gathering bowls. "Time to make those pies or we won't have anything to show for our morning."

Melanie stood at the door looking into the sunshine, yet seeing only memories play through her mind. A family restored. She hadn't thought of that possibility in years. Now she feared that would be the only thing she'd think about.

"What color? Tan or black?" Jason poked at the display of hats on the rack.

"A man doesn't buy a hat because of the color. He has to try it on, shake it around, see if it fits his personality."

"I like your hat and it's black."

"If I thought plaid suited my style, I'd be wearing plaid."

Jason giggled. "And a skirt and that bagpipe thing to go with it?"

Gabe grinned. "Maybe." He reached for a tan hat that looked like it would fit Jason. "Here, let's have a look at you."

Jason studied himself in the trifold mirror. Hamming it up, he struck pose after pose. "Whadya think?"

"I think that second stack of pancakes overstoked your fires."

"They were good." Jason patted his belly as he shuffled back and forth.

Nothing like a full gullet. Gabe removed his hat and ran his hand through his hair. "Glad you're having a good time. Your mom was worried that you wouldn't."

"Mom always worries." He tipped the hat and tried to look at himself sideways in the mirror. "I'm glad we broke our truck here. Mom's having a good time, too."

"Is she? How can you tell?"

"She's sleeping at night."

Gabe perked at the comment as he settled his hat back in place. "She doesn't sleep at home?"

Jason shook his head. "She gets up and walks around the house. Sometimes I peek out my door and see her out on our porch, just sitting." He walked over to the rack and chose a darker tan hat.

"Maybe she has work on her mind."

Jason scrunched up his face. "I hate her job. I'm glad she's looking for another one."

Did Melanie feel the same? His heart picked up a beat. "Why?"

"All she does is work. Lots of times she doesn't even make it home for dinner. Our neighbor Mrs. Wilmer is okay, but all I do at her house is watch TV." He tipped the brim down and tilted his jaw in Clint Eastwood fashion.

Guilt washed over him. "I'm sorry I've asked your mom to work for me, too."

"That's different. It's fun putting the picnic together. She even likes helping at the hardware store." Jason looked up and tipped the hat back. "I don't know why she didn't look for a different job before. Work just makes her sad."

Anticipating an answer he didn't want to hear, Gabe swallowed with effort. "Maybe your mom is seeing someone special?"

"Mom doesn't date. She's just funny that way." Jason scooted over, lifted a black hat off the rack and adjusted it on his head. He tipped his chin this way and that. Pulling the brim low on his brow, he thumped it back until a good measure of his forehead shown. "What do you think about this one?"

Relief a mile wide slid off his shoulders. Gabe inspected the finished product. "Looks good. How about you?"

Jason tugged at it again. "I like it."

"Sold. Now, we need boots."

They repeated the same drill with the boots. As Jason stomped around the wooden floor trying on pair after pair, Gabe stood by the rack. What made Melanie Hunter such a puzzle? A young, beautiful woman, quirky sense of humor, dedicated mother, smart as a whip.

Unsettled, unpredictable, unattached.

His stomach tightened and his vision grew fuzzy as he remembered the kiss they'd shared.

Unattached.

"Gabe, what do you think about these?"

Jason's voice bounced through his thick brain. "How do they feel?"

"I'll need to break them in."

Jason stood in front of the mirror, doing a funky step to see his boots from every angle. Gabe chuckled at the satisfaction he saw on the boy's face. The mountains agreed with Jason. Running around with Fletcher and riding horses, fishing in the stream and riding a four-wheeler. The kid was having a great time.

Unfortunately, so was Gabe.

He had invoices and reports waiting for him back at the office, not to mention the welding on the gate before the auction. The last thing he needed was to daydream about Melanie.

Melanie filled his thoughts all day long.

* * *

Fletcher burst into a barking frenzy as Grace lifted a pie from the oven and placed it on the cooling rack. "It's just Gabe come home."

Melanie scrubbed at red berry stains on her fingernails. Her heart flipped at the casual way Grace talked about her son. When had seeing Gabe become more than commonplace for her?

Way before he'd kissed her.

She flicked the water off her skin and examined her nails. Still pink. Oh well, it showed she'd been working. She grabbed the dish towel and wiped up around the sink.

She sniffed the air. "Nothing like home baking." She wiped her palms before taking the last pie to the oven for baking. They'd rolled, cut, shaped, filled and baked ten pies that morning. And they still had a bowl of berries left over just for snacking.

One pie sat on the cleaned kitchen table. Her pie. Waiting for everyone to taste.

Please Lord, let Gabe like raspberry.

Footsteps pounded up the yard walk. Jason exploded into the kitchen sporting hat, boots and belt. He paraded into the room, his chin held high. "Mom, look what Gabe got for me."

Flicking the brim back and then reseating the hat back onto his head, Jason scrunched up his face in a comical frown, much like the one Martin wore when frustrated. He didn't hold it long before a grin spread from ear to ear. "And look, boots!" He twisted his foot one way then another, making sure he showed his prize off in the best possible light.

Melanie examined him, stirring her finger in the air for him to turn around. "You look terrific, big guy."

"Wait, that's not all." Jason ran to the door just as Gabe and another boy entered. "Look what we got." He peeled off his hat. Gabe did the same.

"Haircuts?" She gaped at the miracle and stared at Gabe. "How did you talk him into it?"

"I didn't have a thing to do with it. I needed the haircut, so we went to the barbershop. Ted let Bud climb on the chair and pumped him up to mirror height. No one talked him into it. He asked for a cut, too. We got shaved and everything."

She sniffed the air again. Same scent as Gabe's, only the aftershave clung to Jason in a thick cloud. "Lather, too?"

"Ted Deacon does the best job in town when he's not distracted." Grace tapped Jason on the shoulder. "Glad you came home with your ears, young man."

"Uh-huh. Mr. Deacon has this strap thing attached to the chair. He wiped the razor on it to make it sharp. But look, neither of us got cut."

"My dad cuts everyone's hair." Wyatt Deacon took off his own hat and modeled his cut. Melanie had seen him at church and at the swing pit. All the boys had welcomed Jason into the fold.

Her gaze locked with Gabe's. The rough planes of his jaw were shaved smooth. Her fingers itched to touch his skin, his hair, everything. "Ted did a good job."

His dimple deepened as his cheeks colored. "Been doing it this way for years."

He settled his hat back in place just as Melanie felt her willpower slip. The dark curls that had fringed his hat before now teased the top of his collar. She looked from man to boy, and smiled.

Jason wore a black hat and light brown boots. Just like Gabe.

Jason eyed the table. "Pies?"

Grace grabbed a hand towel and shook it. "These pies are for Saturday. No chowing before then."

"At all?" Wyatt walked his fingers dangerously close to the end pie.

"Well, maybe in an hour we'll have one pie here ready for

tastin'." Both boys ducked as Grace shooed them away. "Now, go play while they cool."

They shot out of the kitchen without being told twice. Gabe rubbed his hand over his face as if the smooth texture was foreign. "Wasted enough time this morning. Time to start hauling things around. Tell me what you need done next."

"There's a big ol' tractor sitting where the barbecue smoker is going to sit." Melanie pointed to the bare spot of ground not too far from the tree line. "Think you can move that monster and set up the grills?"

"I suppose so." Gabe rolled his words in a lazy answer.

"Great." She leaned her hip against the door. "I have to make sure this picnic goes smoothly."

"I have no doubts about that." Circling the table in a slow stalk, he stuck his hand out to break off a little of the crust. "Umm, raspberry?"

The towel snapped clean, right on his wrist. Gabe jerked back and frowned.

"No tasting for an hour." Grace wrapped the towel up for another flick. "Understand?"

"Yes, ma'am." He rubbed his skin and walked back to the door. "So, Melanie. Want to see the world from the top of a John Deere? You can drive."

"You've seen me drive and you're still offering?" She squeezed through the doorway that Gabe casually filled. Her skin tingled as she brushed his solid chest. "Denting the grill of my pickup cost me a couple weeks of indentured work. What's it going to cost me when I wreck something as tall as a skyscraper?"

"Not a problem." His breath tickled her ear as she passed. "The Deere's got autopilot."

Melanie didn't know if he was joking or not, but she grinned anyway. "Good, because I left my driver's license in the cabin."

They headed for the tall green-and-yellow piece of farm

equipment holding court over a pen of machinery underlings. Tractors, mowers, trailers and other assorted pieces stood in rows, soaking up the summer sun. How did ranchers keep track of what to use for what? She stepped up beside the wheel of the beast, the rim of the tire inches above her head.

Gabe stood beside her. "Climb up the ladder and slide into the cab."

Hiking her foot to get in the first rung, Melanie scrambled up the ladder, Gabe right behind her. She opened the door and dragged herself into the cab. Gabe swung in beside her.

Since the tractor offered only one seat, Melanie pressed against Gabe for balance, her foot wedged against the cab wall. Muscles in his forearm worked as he slammed the door shut. The powerful engine rumbled beneath her feet.

"Look at this view." Gabe leaned back in the seat. With a finger he pointed out over the pasture, trees and peaks. "How can anyone say God didn't have a hand in this?"

Sunshine poured in through the glass cab. "It's beautiful."

"Glad you like it." He shifted to give her more room, draping an arm across the back of the seat. "You ready?"

Melanie bit her lip, hoping her grin didn't make her look a fool. "Full speed ahead."

Chapter Sixteen

Driving the Deere came as natural as casting a fishing line. Gabe steered around a boulder, making note to come back and remove it from the field. "The Fourth of July is usually a weekend of reunions, but I doubt if Nick or Zac will make it to the auction. Too bad—the folks would really like to see both of them."

"Your brothers?"

Not a topic he generally wanted to pursue, but at her spark of interest, he'd give anything to have that gentle voice continue to wrap around him. "Let's see, it's almost July, so Nick is in the thick of rodeo season. He'll be a contender in the NFR again this year."

"NFR?"

"National Finals Rodeo. The biggest rodeo event of the year. Nick's qualified the last two years. Plans on winning overall this year."

She settled deeper in the seat and leaned closer. The lemon scent of her shampoo surrounded him. He could drive the tractor all day.

"And your other brother?"

"Zac loves life in the city." Gabe shifted gears. "Never knew anyone as anxious to leave Hawk Ridge as my little brother, Isaac. Actually, he's not so little. He's the same age as Jennifer, two years younger than me. They went to school together. Jennifer did everything she could to make him notice her, but Zac had no intentions of being saddled in a nothing little town." He didn't want to mention Jennifer wore braids and oversized work shirts as a teen. Zac ran after girls in snug jeans and big hair. "Zac runs the operation from Denver."

"I thought you ran the ranch."

"I run the ranch, but Zac's our front guy. Keeps his finger on the trends of ranching." Gabe shook his head, always marveling at how Zac juggled all the assets. "I tell him where we're going. He tells me how to get there. Works pretty well."

"Is he married?"

Gabe shook his head. "Single and lovin' the life. Mom hates it. She hates Nick staying away, too. But too many memories here on the ranch keep him from coming home."

"Aren't too many rodeos around here anyway, right?"

"He only started riding bulls again after his wife died."

She looked up at him. "I heard. I'm so sorry."

Sunlight filtered through the windshield bathing her smooth cheek. She tilted her head to listen to him, a faint line forming between her brows.

Just keep talking, Davidson.

"Since she died, he avoids the Circle D like the plague. His sending back cattle for the auction is the only connection we have with him anymore. The separation is killing Mom. She thinks it's her fault. But it's not. Nick's just bitter over the hand life dealt him. Dad keeps his nose out of Nick's life, and Mom prays the good Lord keeps her eldest safe until she can make amends."

Gabe let the tractor choose its course as they swept a wide circle in the field. She sat up straighter and studied the valley pasture.

"How in the world can anyone not love it up here? It's beautiful, it's warm, it's quiet. I never thought I'd say it, but I'm going to have a hard time leaving." Her long lashes lowered as she squinted against the sun. A smile tugged at her mouth. "And I was the one who didn't want to stay."

I didn't want you to, either. "Hawk Ridge isn't for everyone."

She tilted her chin and searched his face. "Is Hawk Ridge for you?"

He looked over the fields, trees and mountains. He'd die if he ever had to leave. This was where he was born; this was where he wanted to live out his days. "Me? I'm just too lazy to ever leave home."

"Lazy? Are you kidding me? You're the hardest-working man I've ever met. And the most patient. You always make time for Jason." She stopped her tirade and took a deep breath. "None of my friends take time for Jason except when he's with me. I can't begin to tell you how much I've appreciated the attention he's gotten from you and Hank and everyone up here."

Her lips moved and all Gabe could think about was kissing her. Again. He'd been thinking about it nonstop. Sunshine heated the air, filling his senses with her silky-soft hair. Her cheek just inches from his, he leaned closer until their shoulders touched. He guided the tractor into place along the fence line and let it idle. He reached out and rubbed her cheek.

He angled her chin up and studied her perfect profile. Beautiful, creamy skin. Finely shaped brows and a straight nose.

Her breath stilled. He moved closer until his lips brushed hers. "May I kiss you?"

Sunlight sparkled in her eyes. "You remembered to ask."

He brushed his lips over hers, the sweet softness enough to test his restraint to the limit. As she pressed closer and sighed, her lashes fluttered closed. He kissed her with all the tenderness in his heart. Her sigh told him he'd accomplished his mission. She pulled back.

His heart rate accelerated. What happened? He studied

her rosy cheek as she looked out the window, her lips pressed together. "Melanie?"

A smile played on her lips—a smile creating a beckoning light in her eyes.

"Umm. Thank you." She motioned toward the door. "I think I better go check on those pies."

Sammy's Burger Hut is hiring. I've waitressed before. Melanie strolled down the path with her nose in the sweet, warm air. Insects buzzed around, and layers of pine needles cushioned her steps. This was what she needed. More sunshine and less stuffy office.

A root caught her toe and she stumbled, knocking her out of her daydream. Get real. She considered supporting herself and Jason solely on a small-town waitress job? Melanie didn't need a new office. She needed a few hours of sleep. Since the time Gabe had kissed her, she hadn't been able to think of anything else. She needed a change, but she needed to make that decision with a clear head. She was just worn out.

She came to the bottom of the path and turned toward the ranch house. Fletcher ran across the yard, Jason on his heels. Gabe poked out the kitchen door, throwing a football toward Jason. Jason missed by a long shot, but Fletcher had his back and retrieved the ball, careful to keep it away from both Gabe and Jason. Gabe's full-bodied laughter rang through the air.

Butterflies wearing spurs took flight in Melanie's stomach.

His sleeves rolled to the elbows, Gabe swooped on the dog. Fletcher dodged the hit. Jason circled wide, running to cut off any escape. Gabe scrambled up the center. Fletcher weighed his options. Jason closed in; Gabe swung around.

Fletcher swiveled around and jumped the fence behind him to victory.

Gabe bent over to catch his breath.

Weary though she was, Melanie couldn't deny the scene

before her pulled at her heart. She'd spent the entire night playing Gabe's kiss over in her mind. Each time she melted against him.

Heart pounding, she drank in every detail of the man playing with her son. Even in work clothes, Gabe looked better than any man she'd ever met in the office. She doubted he was even aware of how attractive he was. And playing football with a dog and child? Melanie couldn't think of anything sweeter.

Tears spilled over and down her cheeks before she knew what was happening. When she hiccupped for air, she knew there was no stopping the waterworks.

She pivoted on the spot and marched into the thick of pines.

The river where they'd spent the afternoon that first Sunday gurgled in the distance. Pine needles crunched beneath her feet as flies buzzed around her head and the occasional gnat dived into her lip balm. Pushing aside the last bough, she sidestepped down to the bank.

The water appeared lower than the last time she'd been there. Rapids formed between the rocks out in the middle of the river, leaving calm ponds along the edges. She tore off her shoes and socks and stuck her feet off the edge of the bank, the cold water splashing between her toes. She closed her eyes and listened to the rush of the current. *Lord, I've been away too long. Please forgive me. What am I supposed to do?*

Tipping her face to the sun, she relaxed beneath the warm rays. A soft breeze played with her hair. A light spray of water moistened her face.

What do I do, Lord?

"Quiet and peaceful, isn't it?"

Melanie jumped at the unexpected voice. Her eyelids popped open as she caught her balance. "What are you doing here?"

Gabe stood about ten feet away, his arms folded across

his chest. “Remember our last conversation about not going anywhere by yourself?”

“I’ve been here before. I thought you couldn’t go off into uncharted territory.”

“If I hadn’t followed you, we wouldn’t have known you knew where you were.”

He kept a straight face. Her shoulders tensed as he continued to stare at her. She hadn’t meant to worry anyone.

The familiar dimple appeared. “Have to keep an eye out all the time.”

She relaxed. *I’ll bet you do.* She turned back to the river. “I just needed time to think. To be alone.”

“Fine.”

She heard gravel crunch behind her, then listened as he found a seat. She frowned. What part of wanting to be alone didn’t he understand? “I came here for quiet.”

“You won’t even know I’m here.”

She closed her eyes again. *Lord, how can I pray with him here? I’d like to talk, just You and me.* The echo of rushing water filled her ears. The breeze continued to flutter her hair across her face.

In the gentle spray of river mist, she didn’t think one teardrop would appear too obvious. Maybe one tear from each eye. Why now? She’d had life all figured out. It wasn’t a bad life, was it? Why was normal slipping through her fingers?

Two tears became a torrent. Gentle hands cupped her shoulders and turned her away from the river to a solid chest that smelled like summer sun. His solid support melted her resolve.

“They don’t even know he exists,” she hiccupped between sobs. “My parents have a grandson they don’t even know about.”

He rubbed her back, making her sobs come harder. He shouldn’t be nice to her. He wasn’t going to be so nice when she told him the whole story. Her arms encircled his waist.

“My folks wanted me to put him up for adoption. The

inconvenience, the gossip, was all they'd worried about." The fights and accusations still rang through her head.

"Paul wanted me to get rid of him. When I said no, he dumped me. Just like that. Poof." She squeezed Gabe tighter, the memory of the nastiness making her sick. "He never claimed Jason—swore he'd prove me lying if I ever tried to come after him." She came up for air. "My best friend started dating him." The humiliation and agony of that betrayal hurt her more than any heartache from Paul.

She smacked her forehead into Gabe's chest. She gave him credit. He hung in there for the whole, unvarnished truth. She'd expected him to run long ago. "I want Jason to have what he's found here—a home, family, love. Instead, all he has is me."

His arms tightened around her. She pressed her ear into his chest, absorbing his strength. "Why can't I be more like you? So strong, so patient, so...so confident. Gabe, I'm too scared to go back and make things right. I'm so weak."

"Shhh. There's nothing to be scared of." His voice rumbled along with his strong, steady heartbeat. "Don't bear such needless pain."

Needless pain? She deserved every ounce of burden on her heart.

"Dear Heavenly Father." His chin rested atop her head. "So much hurt and pain remain buried deep, waiting for Your love and mercy to wash it away."

Praying? He prayed for...her? A muscle twitched in her arm as she held on tighter.

"Dear Lord, only You see the cause, only You know the reason. Fill Your children with the realization of the salvation You bought for us with Your blood, ours for the taking if we just trust You."

Fire ignited in the pit of her belly where only moments earlier a ball of ice sat. Her hands slid down along his warm, solid forearms. She squeezed his hands.

"Fill Melanie with Your peace and fill her with Your understanding. You are bigger than any trouble on this earth. Have mercy, oh Jesus."

"Mercy," she whispered. Standing beside rushing waters, her soul cried for cleansing. As her confession of sin, fear, doubts and everything else silently poured out of her, light and relief filled in. After crying her eyes out earlier, she didn't think she had any tears left, but she did.

So much hurt and suffering she'd borne alone. Anger rose in him as he tightened his arms around her. He'd ask forgiveness for judging later as a deeply buried vocabulary exploded in his head toward the man who'd earned her love and trust and then cruelly crushed it into the ground.

Fierce protectiveness shot through his veins. Melanie had dealt with difficult situations and made hard choices all by herself. Decisions she should never have faced in the first place.

Gabe held on as Melanie mumbled words, interrupted by sobs, hiccups and sniffs. Years of hurt and pain flowed out. He hadn't known if he was doing the right thing by following her. He just didn't want her getting lost.

He rubbed his cheek in her soft hair. Her impression of his life was a lie. He should probably tell her, but why be selfish for the sake of unloading his conscience? He wasn't strong. He wasn't independent. He just did what needed to be done.

He'd never had the desire to leave, to make his own mark in the world. He still looked to his father for advice, for direction. *Her* weak? She was the strongest person he'd ever met.

In his world, everyone else did the leaving. He picked up the pieces and held things together best he could. He was no hero. But for now, he'd let her cry on his shoulder and look at him like he was a knight in shining armor.

At the end of the week, she'd be leaving him, too.

* * *

She stared at her cell phone.

Snap it open, punch in the numbers, hit Send.

Melanie reached for her glass of lemonade and took a long drink. With stiff fingers, she opened the phone and entered the numbers. She brought the glass to her lips again.

Her thumb rubbed the Send button.

One more drink.

Send.

The ring came through, indicating the connection made. A lump stuck in her throat. Lord, what am I going to say?

Three rings. Four rings. Five—

"Hello?"

"Dad?" The name flew out of her mouth. "It's me."

Silence thickened like Grace's gravy. "Melanie? Are you all right?"

Her shoulders grew stiff all the way up her neck at his fearful tone. "I'm fine, Daddy. How are you?"

An audible sigh shuddered across the connection. "Fine. Mother's Day was a few Sundays ago. We tried to call you."

Mother's Day? How could she have forgotten? "Sorry, Dad. I've been gone the last few weeks. Guess I lost track of time." What an understatement. "And you?"

"Things just don't change around here. I've been golfing and your mom's been busy with foundation work. She's in the middle of planning a big fundraiser. Been keeping her busy. Wait a second. Ester, come here!" A muffled conversation sounded through the covered mouthpiece. "Talk."

"Hello?" Her mother's puzzled voice came on the line.

"Hi, Mom. It's me."

"Melanie! Are you hurt? Are you in trouble? Do you need anything?" She stopped and caught her breath. "Mother's Day was a few weeks ago."

Comic relief of sorts loosened her back muscles. Mom

hadn't changed. "I'm really sorry about missing it, and no, nothing's wrong. I just wanted to hear your voices."

Her mother's silent reaction lengthened about as much as her father's had. "You do? I don't know what to say."

It felt good to slip into the familiar. "Um, I was wondering. I'm finishing up a project in a couple of days and was wondering if we could come by the house. I want to introduce you to someone."

"We?" Her squeal practically jumped across the airwaves. "Melanie! You're bringing home a boyfriend?"

She winced. "Not exactly."

"Oh."

Her heart fell. Nothing had changed, absolutely nothing. She drew a deep breath. "Mom, I'd like you to meet your grandson."

Chapter Seventeen

Gabe stared at the double-blank domino he'd just drawn. *That's fifty points I'll be stuck with if Jason goes out.* The competitive nature he normally reserved for four-wheeling and mud driving reared its ugly head. The kid tweaked his luck in this game of Mexican Train.

"I only have one more, Gabe." Jason tapped his last piece on the tabletop.

"Well, you win some, you lose some, I guess." Gabe dropped his double-blank right on top of Jason's single. He shrugged. "Sorry, I can't cap it."

Jason's jaw dropped. "Hey, you planned that."

"I didn't know what numbers I'd pull, sport. That's why they call it a *game*."

A knock sounded at the door as Gabe reached for another tile. Still couldn't cap the blank. "Come in."

Melanie stepped in. She looked worn out, her smile not quite reaching her eyes. She searched the room. "Are you guys the only ones here?"

Jason leaned over and took a tile from a spot close to Gabe's elbow. "I was just beating Gabe at dominoes."

"The young man counts chickens before they hatch." Gabe studied her. "You okay?"

She gave a slow nod. "Jason? After the barbecue is over, how about we drive to Denver on Sunday and visit with your grandparents?"

The domino dropped from between his fingers, hitting the oak table with a loud click. "What?"

"Your grandparents. My mom and dad."

Grace walked into the kitchen with her empty glass. She lifted her brow at Melanie, never missing a step to the sink. "Now that sounds nice. Where do they live?"

"South Denver. I grew up in Ken-Caryl Ranch. They never moved."

"Hmm." Grace placed her glass in the sink.

"Your mom and dad? *My* grammy and grandpa?" Jason lost all interest in the game. "I have grandparents?"

The escalading emotions made Gabe uneasy. After the meltdown of yesterday, he certainly didn't think Melanie's life needed scrutiny now. "Hey, Bud. You won three games out of five. That calls for a celebration. How about we run down to the ice cream shop and get double scoops?"

"Sure!" He hopped off his chair. "I want both of them chocolate."

"Melanie, want to come?"

Running her finger along the edge of the table, she didn't meet his gaze. "Why not?"

Gabe grabbed his hat and keys, and herded them toward a black extended-cab pickup around the side of the office. Opening the passenger door, Jason scrambled in, followed by Melanie. Gabe whistled as he rounded the hood, got in on his side and revved the engine. Since he always drove the ranch vehicles, she'd never ridden in his truck before. It was about time.

Country music filtered in through the speakers. Jason jabbered about all the possibilities surrounding his now having grandparents. Melanie sat quietly, giving her son plenty of "uh-hums" in all the right places. Something about the call hadn't gone well. He'd give her time and let her talk when she wanted to talk. He just prayed it wouldn't be an explosion of tears like yesterday.

The starry night surrounded them. He loved these summer nights where the moon shone so brightly you could drive into town without your lights on. Almost. He ambled along the country road, conscious of the deer and elk that might stray into his path.

They got to downtown Hawk Ridge in ten minutes. He parked a block away from the ice cream shop and they all piled out. Jason ran ahead, leaving the two adults in the dust.

"Perfect night for a treat." Gabe strolled along, letting her set the pace. He wasn't in a hurry. "Jason should learn to celebrate all his successes."

"That's never been a problem for him." She looked up with a faint smile. "It's discerning the ones worth celebrating."

Their shoulders bumped. Her smooth arm brushed his. He hooked her little finger with his. She curled into his hand and buried her knuckles in his palm. "It's a good night for you to celebrate, too. The barbecue and auction. They're coming together great. You should be proud."

She smiled up at him, a sad longing in her eyes. "Time has really flown."

Inside the ice cream shop they found Jason perched on one of the stools, pointing to the kind of cone he wanted. Ed kidded him about the size of the waffle cone, but Jason assured him he wouldn't have a problem finishing it.

Gabe ordered two strawberry cones and urged Melanie outside to the tables set up in front of the shop. Traffic was light on Main Street. People usually did what he had done, parked a block away and enjoyed the stroll around town.

Melanie purred as she took a big bite of her ice cream, pulling out a huge chunk of strawberry with her teeth. "No ice cream I've ever had beats this. Glad we're celebrating." She stared at him over her cone and gave him a real smile.

His heartbeat danced even as a blanket of dread covered him. In a short two weeks, he'd gone from his orderly, in-control life to jumping each time he heard her voice and forever checking around to catch a glimpse of her.

Saturday afternoon was the barbecue.

Saturday night she'd get her truck back.

Sunday she'd drive out of their lives.

What was life like before she'd barged in? He couldn't remember, but he had a feeling it was going to be mighty lonely after she left. The same old life stretched before him into eternity. Suddenly, work lost all appeal.

"So you talked to your folks?"

She nodded, keeping her eyes on the ice cream. "It's time. They need to know the truth. They may never forgive me, but they should have a chance to meet Jason."

"Are you okay with this?"

"I guess we'll find out. I just don't want Jason getting hurt."

His gut wrenched at the thought of either of them getting hurt.

"Hey, you guys!" Jennifer waved from across the street. "I want to show you something."

Melanie looked at him like he was the only friend she had on earth before waving to Jen. "She's really sweet, Gabe. You've got great friends."

Yeah, great friends.

"How's the hardware store treating you?" Jennifer dragged a chair to the table. "Mr. Leon told my dad the lawn and garden business has never been better. Guess folks in town like talking to someone who has the right answers about their grass and plants."

"I've only filled in a few days. I like talking plague and pestilence when I know how to fix problems." Melanie took another bite of her cone and then held it out. "Want a bite?"

Jennifer shook her head. Her eyes lit up as she scooted

closer. "Guess what? I took your advice about following my dreams." She placed a brown envelope on the table. "Dad has his doubts about this, but I don't. I'm accepting enrollment in the University of Colorado in Denver for their advanced nursing program. I'm going to earn a master's degree!"

"Nursing school? In Denver? I thought you wanted to try something like a new job here in town." Melanie sat with her eyes wide and mouth open. "I didn't know you wanted to leave."

"Not forever, but if I don't do this now, I'll never have the opportunity again. I'd applied last year and received acceptance for the fall term. I prayed about what road to take and I think God answered my prayer the day we were working on the barbecue arrangements. He sent you to help me make my decision."

As Jen gave Melanie a hug, Gabe felt the earth fall out from under his feet. Jennifer leaving? He thought she'd be here forever. Like Ed Bergin, and Ted Deacon. Mom and Dad and Hank.

Him.

"Isn't this great, Gabe?" Jen pulled away from Melanie. "I'm going to the same medical school as my dad!"

"Great." He managed to move his cone before she engulfed him in a hug.

"I've wanted this for so long. I can't believe it's coming true." She grabbed the envelope. "I've got to get home. Early morning in the clinic tomorrow. I better get used to it." With a smile as bright as the streetlight overhead, she waved and took off toward her car.

"Wow." Melanie caught strawberry ice cream as it rolled down her cone. "I thought all we'd talked about was my finding a new job. I didn't see that one coming."

Neither did he. Jennifer following her dreams? Was that what Nick and Zac had done?

Didn't he have any dreams? Why didn't he leave Hawk

Ridge like everyone else? He'd spent four years going to school at Western State in Gunnison, a drive of only two hours away. At times, even that seemed too far when the snow blew and he knew his dad needed help feeding. So many animals to care for, so much work to do.

He loved every moment of it.

"Whatcha thinking about?" Her cone wavered in front of her chin as she plucked another berry from the ice cream with her teeth.

The gold flecks in her blue eyes danced as she swooped down for another bite and a trail of ice cream dripped down her chin. Her laugh ignited his soul, sparking the realization he'd never met anyone like Melanie, and chances were he never would again. He reached across the table and dabbed her chin with his napkin, her hand coming up to cover his as he swiped at her cheek. He froze, the warmth of her skin on his leaving an indelible mark on his brain.

He didn't want her to leave. "Nothing stays the same, does it?"

"If it did, I never would have met you." Her soft voice knocked him off-kilter like a twelve-gauge load ripping apart a clay pigeon. She'd taken a leap of faith to follow her dream, and he was just a stop on her journey to a new and better life. Especially now with her parents back in the picture. Her life was coming together.

All he had was a cattle operation with more chores than hours in a day. She deserved so much more. And he prayed she'd find it.

Drawing back his hand, he tapped his cone to hers. "Here's to life's changes."

She tapped back. "May they always be for our own good."

As Melanie licked at a drip of ice cream, Gabe looked at his melting cone, suddenly losing his appetite.

* * *

Thursday dawned dark and drizzly. Though the mountains needed the moisture, this wasn't the kind of weather invited to the party. Melanie swept the office floor just as the coffeemaker hissed its completion. Her finishing touches included a vase of wildflowers on the desk and a tray of cookies beside the coffee cups. She wouldn't claim cleaning at home was a pleasure, but straightening out Gabe's office had been fun.

She grabbed a couple of mugs and a thermos from the cabinet and headed out to the corrals. Gabe had left during breakfast to unload the last of the cattle for auction. He hadn't had time to finish his coffee.

Holding her jacket together with one hand and the thermos and cups in the other, she picked her way across the muddy drive then wiped her boots on the grass edging at the front of the corrals. The truck and trailer stood empty. Following the fence, she ducked into the dark interior of the black barn.

RJ stood on the rails of the fence calling out instructions to the driver, who waved his arms at the animals to make sure they didn't retreat. Gabe stood in one pen encouraging the angry bovine to enter the other; the rain and mud weren't helping their cause.

Melanie set the cups and thermos down on a bale and stepped closer to the rail where Hank stood. Gabe danced in the corral, anticipating every move until the first animal snorted and ran into the pen. Finally the others made it in the correct pens. The men stood back and applauded.

"That's the last of 'em, Gabe." RJ stepped off the rail. "Nick really came through."

"He sure did. Sorry he won't be at the auction for the folks around here to tell him how much they appreciate everything." Gabe climbed over the panel. "Wouldn't hurt for Nick to hear it for himself."

"He will someday." Hank swiped mud from his jeans. "He will."

Melanie uncapped the thermos and filled the cups. She wished she had more time to get to know the people of Hawk Ridge. What was Nick like? Or Zac? Some questions were probably better left unanswered. It was bad enough they were leaving the folks of the Circle D. If she'd had more time to get to know the town, she'd be in big trouble.

"Hi guys." She waved. "Since you didn't finish your coffee inside, I thought I'd bring it out to you."

"Thoughtfulness is your middle name, Melanie Hunter." Hank accepted the first mug. "I appreciate it."

RJ ambled up, his wet hat in his hand. He nodded and reached for his cup. "Thanks. Gotta warm a guy up on a day like this."

"You're welcome." She reached for another cup. Angling around, she handed Gabe a mug.

"Thanks. That's the last load." He rewarded her with a smile that sent the gloomy feeling of the day out the stall door. "Now to number them off and we're all set."

Hank lifted his mug in the direction of the house. "I'm raiding the kitchen for a cinnamon roll to push down this coffee."

"If I go in there, I won't come back out." Gabe kept his attention on her. "We've got bulls and cattle to auction off…"

She listened to him talk with only half an ear. Standing there a dripping, muddy mess, she'd never seen anyone finer than Gabe Davidson. She'd fallen in love with the last person she ever wanted to even like. For his strength and steadfastness. For his love of God, the mountains and his affection for her son. For his patience and humor with her.

She'd resisted acknowledging her feelings. The relationship would never work. A man as vibrant and strong as Gabe Davidson didn't belong in the city, and she didn't know the first thing about ranching to be helpful here. No one would win.

"...And that will probably end our day until the loading starts. That's another issue. I'll be glad when it's over."

Hank scooted through the door. "C'mon, RJ. Hot biscuits and honey to go with the cinnamon rolls. Don't mind the sugar rush when it's fresh out of the oven." The men left, discussing the merits of honey vs. molasses on a hot biscuit.

The barn fell silent except for the gentle snorts of tired animals. Rain pattered in the mud puddles and *ting*ed off the metal roof of the shed outside. Melanie swiped the hair out of her eyes. She couldn't think of any place she'd rather be than right here. "This has been such an experience for all of us. Thanks for roping me into it, Gabe."

His gaze softened and he tipped his hat back. "The pleasure was all mine."

She stepped up beside him, her knuckles grazing his Carhartt jacket. "I'm going to miss all of this."

He leaned closer. "All of it?"

His breath tickled her ear. "All of it."

His lips brushed hers. All the fantasies she'd ever had rolled through her mind. She leaned back and drew a breath.

"I just wanted you to know, I've never *wanted* to kiss a man more than I do you."

The desire in his eyes made the gold pattern in the rich brown deepen. He regarded her for a long moment, and Melanie feared she'd stepped too far. Then a grin lifted the corner of his mouth and his ever-so-familiar dimple deepened.

Blood pumped through her veins again, only this time with a strong, steady beat. She moved closer until his strong arms wrapped around her.

His breath warmed her cheek. "You are such a gift."

She tilted her chin until their lips met. For so many years, she'd avoided any closeness or thought of a relationship. But Gabe made her forget her resolve. He made her think of possibilities she only dreamed. Gabe lived the love in his eyes.

Melanie would cherish that revelation to her grave. It would be a long time before she'd allow herself to trust anyone as she did Gabe. If ever. All she wanted was a taste of what she'd be walking away from.

Thank you, Lord, for this last time.

She broke away first, the sweet pressure of his lips lingering. She read the wonder in his eyes and smiled. "Thanks, Mr. Davidson."

His dimple deepened. "The name's Gabe."

"Thanks, Gabe."

His gaze darted over her face. "I was kinda hoping you might stick around after the party."

Her heart pounded as she warmed from the inside out. *I'd love nothing more.* "I have to go visit my parents."

"Maybe afterwards?" He ran his finger down her cheek.

The splash of mud outside the barn door ruined the moment. Hank walked in with his mug of coffee and a half-eaten cinnamon roll in his hand. "Looks like the skies are clearing up. We can start setting up the pens." He stopped in midchew. "Did I miss something?"

Melanie tried to cover her grin with her hand. She headed toward the door, stopping a few feet past Hank. "Hank? Thanks for everything."

Hank looked from her to Gabe. He swallowed and rewarded her with a sheepish grin. "Glad to be of service."

Jason caught the Frisbee. Fletcher wanted it back. Melanie rushed in for the tackle.

"Mom, you can't do that." Jason wrapped his arms around her leg as she held the plastic disk in the air, ready to throw. "When Fletcher gets it, he doesn't give it back. Noooo."

She flicked her wrist, releasing the Frisbee. Fletcher took off at a dead run. "Jason, it's his toy."

"He doesn't play fair." Jason released her and took off after the dog.

Doubling over, Melanie laughed until her side hurt. Jason

had never had a problem sharing his toys; obviously, Fletcher did. Too bad they couldn't have a dog in their complex back home.

"Melanie," Grace called from the kitchen door. "Telephone for you."

"For me?" She stretched out her side cramp and cocked her head. "Mr. Leon?"

Grace shook her head. "A Ms. Johnson?"

Her heart raced triple time. Melanie hopped onto the porch and found the phone receiver on the kitchen counter. Her palms sweaty, she cradled the phone to her ear. "Hello? This is Melanie Hunter."

"Ms. Hunter? This is Glynna Johnson from the Dean Group in Montrose. We have reopened interviews for the analyst research position. I understand you were not able to attend the initial interview. Are you interested?"

The no-nonsense voice on the other uttered the invitation Melanie thought she'd never hear again. Her stomach knotted. Another chance.

"Yes, very much so." She tried not to sound too eager.

Pages rustled in the background. "Dr. Hillman will be out of the office next week. Would the following Monday fit into your schedule?"

"Yes. Yes, that will be fine."

"I have you down for ten o'clock Monday morning. We look forward to seeing you."

Melanie replaced the phone receiver. Would miracles never cease? God had given her another chance, a new start to build a home.

Thank you, Lord.

She stepped out onto the porch where Grace watered a ceramic pot filled with geraniums. "Grace, you'll never guess what happened."

"What, honey?"

"The position in Montrose hasn't been filled. They called to see if I was still interested. Can you believe it?"

"Are you?" Grace looked up from her watering. "Still interested?"

"Are you kidding me? This job is everything I've ever wanted for Jason. Small town, small schools, simple life." Melanie turned her face to the sky and let the sun kiss her. "The answer to my prayer."

Chapter Eighteen

"I couldn't eat another bite." Melanie pushed from the kitchen table and took her plate to the sink. The morning sun brightened her attitude, considering the barbecue was set to start in a couple of hours. "I think I've gained five pounds in the last few weeks."

"An extra five pounds never looked as good on me." Grace gave her the once over. "If you've got 'em, we can't see 'em."

"Gracie." Martin patted her hand. "In the lean times and in the good, I love every inch of you."

"Oh, go on." She swatted at him.

Gabe cleared his throat. "Didn't sound much like love a couple days ago when Mom put that salad in front of you."

Melanie laughed with them, marveling at how easy it had been to slip into the warmth of the family. She'd never experienced total acceptance, complete inclusion, as she had from the moment they'd rolled onto the Davidson Ranch. *God bless this special place.* A healing place. A place filled with love.

She caught Gabe looking at her, and heat rose to her cheeks. Since the day before last, she'd been walking on air. She'd kissed the most handsome, kind, considerate man she'd ever known. She'd accepted his invitation to return to the ranch after visiting with her folks.

He'd even reassured her of his feelings last night by praying with her at the door of the cabin after he'd walked her home from the evening of movies at his parents'.

Her smile started to fade. Today was the last day she'd be with the family, with Gabe. Tomorrow she'd get her truck back and drive off to introduce Jason to his grandparents. Then she faced the possibility of relocating to a new town, a new life. She drew a deep breath and pulled her smile tighter.

When had her life become so complicated?

"Melanie, how about we spread those tablecloths now?" Grace stacked the breakfast dishes in the sink. "Crowd will be here before you know it."

"Let me run back to the cabin." Melanie stepped away from the counter and started for the door. "I forgot a clip and my hair is going to drive me nuts."

"It looks great." Gabe met her at the door with a grin. He opened the door for her and did a double take. "Someone's here already. They're not supposed to show up until eleven o'clock."

Melanie peeked past his shoulder and saw a midsized sedan with dealer plates at the yard fence. The sun reflected off the windshield. She couldn't see inside no matter how hard she squinted.

Grace came up behind her. "Might as well welcome them. We've still got plenty of waffles and sausage."

Gabe pushed the door open and stepped out. "Mornin', folks. Come for the auction?"

The driver's side door opened and a man with a khaki-colored camper hat got out. A woman with gray, perfectly coiffed hair stepped out of the passenger side. They both looked around at the buildings then back to Gabe. "We're looking for Melanie Hunter."

The blood drained from her face. *No. Not here.* The pit

of her stomach roiled and knotted, and Melanie thought her double stack pancakes would make a return appearance. She grabbed the doorknob as her knees went weak.

"What's wrong?" Grace grabbed her arm. "Come here and sit."

"I'm okay, just…just surprised."

Voices filtered up the walk. Gabe opened the door and let the guests in. "Melanie? Someone here to see you."

She wasn't ready for them yet. Why today? Why now? "Mom. Dad. What are you doing here?"

Jason ran in from where he'd been setting up the dominoes to play with Martin. "Mom? Is someone here for you?"

Ester Hunter sized up the boy as if she were appraising one of her antiques. She looked from Melanie to him, then back at her. Apparently satisfied with what she saw, she offered a strained smile. "We've come to meet our grandson."

Jason stepped closer. "Mom, is this your mom and dad?"

Finally finding her voice, she nodded. "Ester and Jim Hunter, this is Grace and Martin Davidson. And behind you, Gabe Davidson." She cleared her throat as everyone exchanged greetings. All she wanted was for the earth to open up and swallow her. She hadn't anticipated this at all.

Gripping Jason's shoulder, she eased him in front of her. "And this is Jason. Your grandson."

"Hello, young man." Jim Hunter kneeled until he was Jason's height. "You been taking care of your mother all these years?"

"Yes, sir." Jason hesitated. "Nice to meet you, sir."

Her dad smiled the same crooked smile Melanie remembered him giving her. "You've done a fine job."

"Thank you, sir."

Melanie had never heard so many *sirs* out of her son in his life. As her dad straightened, she looked from Ester to Jim and frowned. "What are you doing here? How did you find me?"

Ester nodded at Grace. "Grace called us the other evening and invited us to a barbecue you're hosting. You didn't mention it in your phone call."

Melanie stood speechless. Grace had sold her out.

"What better way to reunite than surrounded by friends," Grace chimed in with her usual good humor. "Littleton isn't that far from here. I thought your parents might enjoy a drive in the mountains on a beautiful summer day."

"And pork flies south for the winter," Martin mumbled behind Melanie, shuffling around until he stood next to his wife. "Jim and Ester, nice to meet you. Why don't we go sit outside while Grace fixes tea? Gabe? Is everything ready for the crowd?"

Gabe nodded. "Nice meeting you, folks." He opened the door and disappeared.

Coward. What was she supposed to do? So many last-minute details needed attention. She didn't have time to catch up on eight years of baby history. That was what tomorrow was supposed to accomplish. Today, she'd had other plans.

Plastering on a smile, she indicated the door. "The table is right around the house."

Gabe walked out the door then shot around the side of the house and came back in the office door. He stood in the living room until Melanie, Jason and her folks were out of hearing. Stalking into the kitchen, he cornered his mother. "What have you done?"

"Nothing that any concerned friend wouldn't have done. I arranged a meeting for Melanie and her parents on neutral territory. Her relationship with her parents is strained. She needed to mend fences someplace where she felt comfortable. With all the party planning on her mind, and now a chance at that job she wants, she hasn't had much time to think through her options. Considering she's leaving for Denver tomorrow, I had to act fast."

"Maybe she wanted to handle this herself?" Anger simmered just beneath boiling. Gabe had stood by and watched his mother orchestrate the lives of his brothers. The result? Both were gone and had few plans on returning. Something deep down told him she had plans for him, too.

"Gabriel Thomas, watch your tone." Her eyes darkened, the only sign of her agitation. "I just had the best interests of that girl in mind. She needs support right now and I hate to say it, but we're it. The last thing I want to see is her running away again and her parents never getting to know that precious boy. They need to talk. Children need to honor their parents."

"And parents respect their children." Gabe fought to keep his voice low.

"Exactly." Martin came up behind Gabe, putting his hand on his shoulder. "On both counts. Grace, go give those people a drink of tea."

Tension strummed between mother and son. The look on her face announced she knew she'd won the battle. She always did. She gathered up tea, glasses and spoons and backed out of the screen door, tray in hand.

"God is stronger and wiser than Grace Davidson and if He wants fences mended, He'll supply the materials Himself." Martin rubbed his chin. "I don't approve of her meddling, son, but she has a point. Melanie is a strong woman when it comes to protecting and providing for Jason. Something tells me she's not quite sure what to do about taking care of herself. Maybe it's good we're here for her."

Of course Dad was right. Too bad his advice didn't remove more of the sting of his mother's methods. Protecting Melanie and Jason beat fiercely within his chest. Gabe stopped and frowned.

Because she'd confided in him?

Because she'd shared her secrets?

Because she made him feel like a hero?

Gabe blinked a couple of times to clear his head. His father stood beside him, watching him with that look on his face. That look told Gabe every cog, every piece, was falling into place and his dad was close to solving the mystery.

Gabe turned on his heel and headed out the back door. He stalked across the open lot and into the barn where his entrance startled the two fat barn cats. He paced down the corridor then retraced his steps. The cats tangled around his feet and he pushed them away.

He liked Melanie. He liked Jason.

He hadn't been paying attention. The truth washed over him and stopped him flat.

He loved them.

Her battle with the taffy popped into his mind. The pure joy on her face as she'd swung high in the air before letting go of the swing. The wracking sobs as he'd held her in his arms and stood by as she poured out the anguish she'd held in her heart for so many years. Had he only known her a couple of weeks? Seemed like forever.

Lord, how can I fall in love with a woman I barely know? One who has her life all figured out and none of her plans include me?

Gabe hung his head and leaned against the stall door. Now he understood a fraction of the pain Nick had undergone when his wife died. If it hurt this much to lose, how would it feel to win?

Hasty footfalls pounded toward the barn. Jason ran past the open doors like a pack of wolves nipped at his heels. Gabe ran out in time to see Jason round the corner and disappear.

Jogging down the side of the barn, Gabe found Jason leaning against the rails of the fence, his head buried in the crook of his arm. "Hey, Bud. The party's this way."

Jason didn't answer. Gabe stepped up and saw the uneven breaths, heard the sniff. Gabe hung his elbows over the fencing and jammed his boot on the bottom rail. "Looks like the day has surprises for everyone."

"I don't like them." Jason kept his arm over his eyes. "They're not like grandparents are supposed to be. They're so stiff. Make them go away."

Hurt emanated from the little body. Betrayal. Gabe understood wanting something to be one way and finding out it's nothing like you'd imagined. *Lord, give me the right words.* "Yep, it's pretty hard meeting someone important for the first time. You don't know how to act. I know if it's someone real important to me, I get all tongue-tied. I'm scared I'm going to say the wrong thing and they won't like me."

Gabe stepped closer and knelt beside Jason, staring eye level at the tear-streaked face. "Always remember, Jason. A good, loving family is the best you can have here on earth. Family will stand by you when things get tough and no matter how foolish you act, they'll always be there to love you."

"Isn't Mom enough?"

"God knows what He's doing." His dad's words of only moments ago rang through his head. "He has a plan for you that can't be derailed. He brings people into your life because maybe there's something you can teach them."

Jason swiped his sleeve across his eyes. "Really?"

Gabe nodded. "Give your grandparents a chance. They're going to love you."

Jason flung himself into Gabe's chest. Gabe caught his balance just before the both of them toppled over. Jason buried his face and rubbed his forehead in Gabe's shirt. "Are you sure?"

Feeling the words thicken in his throat, he hugged Jason tight. "They'll love you more than you'll ever know." *And so do I.*

In the distance, Gabe heard Melanie calling. With a final hug, he pulled just far enough away to look into the uncertain face. "Always remember, Bud. God knows what He's doing."

Melanie rushed around the corner of the barn. "Jason. What

happened?" She pulled him into a hug and then set him back, a serious scowl on her face. "Why did you run?"

Jason kicked at the ground. "I dunno."

The standoff between the two twisted his gut. Gabe rested his arm over Melanie's shoulders and drew Jason close. "Is there not anything we've learned over the past weeks? I don't know about you, but I sure have." He resisted the urge to bury his face in her soft, shining hair. Jason wrapped his arm around his leg and Melanie nestled closer to his side. They stood together as he always prayed someday he would with a family of his own.

"Life is full of surprises. Just when you think you have all the answers, you realize the questions weren't the ones you wanted answered in the first place."

She shifted and looked up at him, her brow raised in question.

"When you guys first showed up, all I thought of was having one more responsibility added to my workload." Melanie tried to squirm away but he held her tight. When her frown deepened, he winked at her.

"When my load began to lighten because you were here, I breathed a sigh of relief. When I started looking forward to seeing you every day, I gave thanks to God for bringing you into my life."

Jason hugged harder. "Gabe, I like seeing you every day, too."

Gabe tightened his embrace around them and thought he felt Melanie rub her cheek on his shoulder. "We've all been through some hefty changes. Bud, your grandparents just want to get to know you. Let them see the real Jason, and I'm pretty sure they'll love you all the more for it."

"He's right, Jason." Melanie cleared her throat. "Mom and Dad haven't met you. But they want to get to know you. They want a chance to love you."

Gabe swallowed against the tightening in his throat. "They

want to get to know you, too, Melanie. Family is a wonderful thing." He squeezed them tight.

Wisps of her soft hair brushed his skin as she turned and kissed him on the cheek. She gave him a watery smile that made Gabe want to hug her and never let her go. Ever.

Melanie sniffed. "C'mon, Jason. Let's go meet the folks."

Melanie walked with Jason and her parents around the grounds, milling with the folks showing up for the barbecue, introducing her parents to the town. She knew something about everyone who greeted them, making the strangers she was introducing to her parents sound like old friends.

"Melanie!"

Jennifer popped up behind Mr. Deacon and waved a bandana in the air.

"Thought I'd never find you. Will you look at this crowd?"

Shayna skirted around a group of men and squeezed past a chair and table. She grabbed Melanie by the arm and pulled her into a hug. "Thanks so much for filling in at the store. I can't begin to tell you how much better I feel. Dad's not as worried about me now."

She stepped back beside Jennifer. "I can't believe how many people are lined up to eat!"

Jennifer craned her neck. "Folks probably knew Gabe had someone else cooking for him, so the food was safe to eat." She winked at Jason.

He giggled. "Gabe made me a baloney sandwich and it was good."

"Yeah, well, he ought probably stick to that specialty of the house." She turned to Jim and Ester. "Jennifer O'Reilly."

"Shayna Leon." She wedged in between Jennifer and Melanie. "Are you here with Melanie?"

"These are my parents." Melanie made the introductions.

"They've come up to see what we've been doing with our summer."

"Great!" Shayna rushed in. "Melanie has helped me so much."

Ester raised an arched brow. "Oh? What did you do?"

"Just offered a friend some support." In such a short time, Shayna and Jennifer had become her friends. A reality Melanie still struggled with. "Doesn't the barbecue smell great?"

"Hank tossed seasoning on the beef to keep up with the spices you rubbed into the pork. RJ is flipping ribs as fast as he can." Jen pointed all around. "Ed, Bob, Gus, all of 'em love it. Guess you know you'll be welcome back anytime."

Melanie stopped before she spoke. The town liked her? All she did was organize a picnic, and really, if truth be told, she didn't do much of the planning. She grinned at Jen for stretching the truth.

"Melanie." Her mother broke through the fog. "Where have you and Jason been living?"

"Over here, Grammy." Jason pointed up the path. "Wanna see?"

A tender smile touched her mother's eyes. "I'd love to."

Jason squeezed between his grandparents and led them up the path. Melanie brought up the rear. Jason's existence was a shock to her folks, and they handled the surprise quite well. Those miracles just kept popping up all over the place. They reached the end of the path and Jason pushed open the door.

"Home." He swung out his arm.

"It's beautiful." Her mother took a quick look around the small cabin. She came back out while Dad and Jason poked around. "The Davidsons were very generous to let you use such a quaint cabin. And look at this view! I'd say it was worth planning the party, wouldn't you?"

The lightness of her mother's voice stunned her. Her mother, the one who always saw life through very proper eyes—teasing her over the situation? Melanie couldn't help but smile back. "Two people and one bathroom in the mornings became dicey at times, but yes, it's been wonderful."

"Seems like many things are wonderful up here."

The mountains, the people, Grace and Martin. Gabe. Yes, a lot about Hawk Ridge was wonderful. "I really like the small town."

Ester tilted her head. "Hmm."

Jason gabbed as he came out of the cabin, tugging his Grandpa by the hand. "And Gabe taught me how to ride a horse, and Hank's teaching me how to rope and..." The two passed Melanie and Ester on their way down to the food.

"Your friends seem nice."

Melanie scuffed her toe into the dirt. "Jennifer is a nurse and Shayna works for her dad in the hardware store. They're very special."

"I can tell." Ester circled around, pushing a pine bough out of the way. "When is she due?"

"Four weeks, I think."

A distant look clouded her eyes. "I'll bet her family can't wait."

"Yeah, her dad is pretty excited."

Ester tilted her head. Melanie knew what her mother's next question would be and she didn't want to discuss it now.

"I guess we better go eat while there's food left." The words flew out of her mouth. Melanie dreaded moments alone with her mother, wanting to put off judgment day as long as possible. "It is, after all, my party."

As she turned toward the path, she felt her mother's hand on her shoulder. Melanie hesitated then met the bright eyes of her mom.

"I'm glad you kept him." Her mother's chin trembled.

Tears stuck in her throat. The memory of the fighting and screaming and all the hurtful words that had shot between herself and her parents wove through her mind. Melanie waited for the familiar stab of resentment and anger…but all she felt was relief.

She managed a smile in return and embraced her mom. "I'm glad. I was so scared you'd find out."

Ester hugged her close. "I'm sorry we made you feel that way." She pulled away and cupped Melanie's face with her palm. "We have a lot to talk about after your event is over."

Chapter Nineteen

The crowd ebbed and flowed around the tables loaded with ribs, burgers, salads, desserts and everything in between. Gabe had never seen so many loaded plates balanced on arms and hands full of cold drinks. The last burden of worry slipped off his shoulders.

Good food, sunny skies, hungry folks. Couldn't ask for a better party.

At the edge of the trees, on the path leading to her cabin, Melanie stood and waved as Jason led her parents toward the buffet line. Gabe knew he'd not find a better chance to apologize for his mother's behavior. In a few hurried steps, he darted around the scrub pine and caught Melanie before she could get away.

"Hi."

Her smile lit her face. She moved closer and snaked her arms around his waist, giving him a squeeze. "Thanks for everything, Gabe. I know I never would have taken the step to make amends with my parents if it hadn't been for you."

His words of apology died on his lips as he wrapped her in his embrace, his blood pumping straight to his head and making him dizzy. "I'm glad everything worked out."

"Not completely. Not yet. But we've got a good start." She

tilted her face up at him and squinted against the sun. "I'm glad you're here. I'm not sure how this would've turned out if I didn't have you and your family as support."

Gabe squeezed her tighter. Okay, so he'd apologize to his mother instead of Melanie. To some degree, he was glad the circumstances had turned. He didn't want to give Melanie a reason to leave. Ever.

"I always want to be here for you." He lowered his head and met her lips, drinking in her sweetness on a sigh. She clutched at his shirt and drew him close, her desperation mirroring his own. He knew he'd stepped past all known boundaries.

He released her lips, but wrapped his arms around her tighter. "When this is all done, and the guests are all gone, we need to talk."

She snuggled her cheek against his chest, her soft hair brushing against his chin. She rubbed her nose on his shirt. "That would be a good idea."

He kissed the top of her head. He didn't know exactly what he was going to say, but he knew she made him complete. The words *I love you* threatened to pour out. He swallowed them, knowing he had to find a better time, a better place, to pour out his heart. "The best."

Pulling out of his embrace, Melanie slid her hand down his forearm and entwined her fingers with his. "C'mon, we've got a party to throw."

They mingled over to the grills. The smell of pork ribs rubbed with mesquite spices filled the air as meat smoked on the racks. His mouth watered. "Hey, great food."

"Nothing like a fine rack of pork ribs at any barbecue," RJ proclaimed with all the satisfaction of a cat finishing a cup of cream. "Gotta keep 'em real tender. Melanie, what do you see over there?"

Gabe followed the direction of the meat tongs to the platters on the long table. Eager people speared forkfuls of tender meat onto gigantic puffs of bread, each bun looking more like a small sheepherder's loaf than a hamburger bun.

She squeezed his hand and grinned. "Happy people?"

RJ gave a quick nod and winked. "The third round of barbecue on that table is almost gone."

Hank clamped a chunk of steak and flipped. "Nothin' wrong with pork or beef sharing the spotlight. It's all in the choices."

"You just wait until next year, cowboy." RJ tipped his hat. "I'll make the best fall-off-the-bone pork ribs you've ever tasted."

"Yer on."

Gabe didn't miss the challenge. "RJ? You're staying?"

The younger cowboy turned back to the grill, giving Gabe a view of tan hat and suntanned hands. "Thought maybe it'd be all right with you if I stuck around."

"You're welcome to stay as long as you want." Gabe gripped his shoulder and looked down at the grill. "Unless you go burning the ribs."

A cheek-splittin' grin was all the answer Gabe needed.

Hank shut the lid and turned toward the table behind him. He lifted two plates heaped with meat, bread and ears of corn. "Here, you two eat. By the time this crowd gets done there won't be nothin' left but the coals."

"Thanks, Hank."

Gabe threaded through the crowd to a side table by the pens. He set the plates down and let Melanie scoot in on the bench seat. He shrugged toward the tables. "Sounds like a happy bunch to me."

She grazed a kiss across his cheek as she reached for a fork. "Everyone's so busy visiting, they'll probably forget all about the auction."

Her breathy voice tickled his ear. He dipped and kissed her back before she took a bite of her rib. "Better not. I don't want a single uninvited bovine left behind."

Pure adoration lit her blue eyes as she laughed and swiped her hands with a napkin. "Where's that ornery bull? Remember, the day we came to the Circle D? The trouble he caused?"

"Yeah well, you'll have that with bulls." Gabe smiled before he took a bite of his barbecue sandwich. The taste of heaven danced through his mouth. With his elbow, he pointed across the pens. "Milk River is over there." He set his food down and wiped his mouth. "What's Bud doing by that pen?"

"Jason's with my parents." She leaned forward. "Is something wrong?"

"Don't know." He rose from the table, never taking his eyes off his target. "Won't know till I get there."

Melanie chased after Gabe, weaving through the gates and pens until she caught a glimpse of what he'd seen. She stopped in her tracks, her breath caught in her throat. Another two pens down, Jason balanced on a fence panel, his face flushed with excitement as he waved to her parents. Jim and Ester walked toward him, Ester making motions for Jason to jump down.

Jason climbed a rail higher and waved harder.

"Jason!" Melanie yelled, though the noise around her all but drowned out her warning. "Get down from there!"

Gabe approached the corner of the pen. As he turned, he called out. Jason looked around and waved at him, too. The white bull paced around his pen, snorting and shaking his head. She looked at the panel in front of her. How did it open? If she could open the pen, the animal would go through the gate, wouldn't he?

"Gabe, you can see all the cattle from up here." Jason looked over the lot, his shins leaning against the top rail. He tipped his cowboy hat back as Melanie had seen Gabe do a thousand times. Jason pointed. "Grandpa look, twenty-five—"

Milk River butted the fence panel Jason stood on. He bent

to grab the top rail but the bull rammed it again. He lunged for the rail and missed. His body disappeared into the pen.

"Jason!" Melanie screamed. She tore around the panels in time to see Gabe vault into the pen.

Conversation stopped and a crowd formed. Hank raced past her. Melanie shoved her way to the front. In the dirt and mud, all she saw was Gabe huddled up and wedged under the bottom rail of the panel. Milk River snorted and butted the panel over Gabe time and again, pawing at the ground as slobber dropped in strings from his mouth.

From beneath the rail, a small hand stuck out. She dove for the ground and clutched his palm to her face. *Oh Lord, save them! Please, save them!*

She repeated the desperate plea over and over. The bull grunted and stepped back. She leaned forward so that her forehead rested against Gabe's shoulder pressed through the rails. *Lord,* do *something!*

The clang of gate panels rang through the air as the animal left the pen, his bellow a blatant cry of victory. Melanie kneaded the small fingers between hers. Before she could say anything, strong hands gripped her shoulders and urged her back. On the other side of the panel, Hank and another man bent over Gabe.

"Come back here, Melanie." She recognized her father's voice. He continued to murmur low to her as he pulled her away from Jason.

She protested, but found she had no strength to match the words.

"Take it easy, honey." He hugged her. "They have someone checking them now."

"Jason…Gabe." She stared in a horrific trance.

They pulled Gabe back and Jason wiggled out from under him. Bruised and dirty, Jason stared at the crowd, wild-eyed. Melanie tore away from her father and scrambled to the fence.

"Mom." Tears streaked down his face. He gulped air as he reached for her. Melanie grabbed on. He dragged his foot out from under Gabe and wiggled through the rail. She gathered him up, checked him over and buried her face in his hair.

Slowly, she became aware of Gabe. He lay so still. Hank helped the other man move him around. Jennifer stood behind them.

"What do you need, Dad? Can we move him?"

Jennifer's dad, the doctor. Melanie devoured their every move with her eyes. Jason sobbed against her. She held him tight. She prayed.

The doctor looked up at Hank and nodded as he talked. Hank stepped aside as Martin squeezed in, Grace right behind him. The pen became crowded with people.

Oh Lord, have mercy on him. Take care of him. Save him.

"Come back here, Melanie." This time her mother spoke over her. She wanted to ignore them all. A gentle hand touched her shoulder. "Let's give them some room."

Melanie allowed her dad to guide them away from the crowd. She squeezed Jason as Martin and Hank hauled Gabe up and made their way to the house. Jennifer and her dad followed as Grace ran ahead. Melanie wanted to follow, to hold Gabe's hand, to stay by his side until he looked up and she could stare into his incredible brown eyes and see for herself he was okay.

"Think of the boy." Jim Hunter sat in her kitchen and lectured Melanie in an all-too-familiar tone. "He's eight years old. Do you know how much trouble he can get into if no one is watching?"

How would she ever forget the mischief Jason got into even when people watched? She checked over her shoulder at the open door of her room where he'd fallen asleep, exhausted.

Melanie shook her head. "I need to stay and make sure everything from the auction is taken care of."

"Will you, just once, listen to reason?" Her mother stood at the kitchen counter, the bulky mug in her hand looking terribly out of the place in her manicured grip. "These people have a tremendous amount of stress to deal with right now. Just come home with us and perhaps, when circumstances die down, you can come back and visit. Button up your personals then."

Melanie stared out the picture window. Somewhere over the last couple of weeks, she'd formed a habit of sitting and looking out the window at the pinecones and moss rocks. Familiar. Comforting. If she looked out the kitchen window, she could see into the valley. Out her bedroom, forest so thick the squirrels could run from tree to tree with little effort.

Back home? The front door of Mrs. Wilmer's town house. "Mom. Dad. I can't just leave."

"You said you were leaving tomorrow anyway." Her mother teetered on the edge of whining. "You and Jason were coming for a visit. Why have your plans changed?"

"I don't know how Gabe is. Martin and Grace will need help cleaning up the grounds. I don't have my truck."

Jim lifted his hand and fanned his fingers. "That young man is sturdy, and I'm certain he'll survive. The parents are mountain people—this isn't their first accident or gathering. If you were getting your truck back tomorrow, it must be ready now." He finished ticking off his reasons, holding his thumb for drama. "Jason is our grandson. We don't want him hurt."

Her father's hand remained in her line of sight. All the old anger and resentment surged through her. All the old hurt.

Every little bit of it.

"*You* don't want him hurt? *You?*" She tried to keep her voice low, afraid of waking Jason. "You never wanted me to keep him. You wanted me to put him up for adoption."

Pressure built in her throat. She squeezed her eyelids tight, feeling the tears run down her cheeks. "Paul just wanted me to get rid of him."

"Honey, we thought we knew what was best."

Melanie opened her eyes and swiped at the tears. Her mother's voice quivered as she drew a chair up to the table. "You were only twenty years old. Raising a child is difficult enough for a couple, let alone a single young woman. We only wanted to help."

"Help? By giving away my baby?" Melanie grabbed a napkin from the holder on the table and blew her nose. "You never even came after me."

Her father rested his elbow on the table and hung his head. "We've known all about Jason."

She looked from parent to parent. The sorrow in their eyes testament to the pain they all shared. "Why didn't you say something?"

"Why didn't *you?*" Her mother reached out and covered Melanie's wet, cold knuckles with her warm palm. "Each time you came to visit, we prayed you'd bring the baby. You never did. It only took a few visits for us to realize how much we'd hurt you. After years went by, what could we say that wouldn't drive you further away?"

"You're an amazing young lady, Melanie." Her father stretched out his hand to her. "Our prayers were answered every day God kept you safe. I never thought we'd have the opportunity to meet Jason, much less call him grandson."

Parents try hard to do the right thing. Wasn't that what Grace had said? Melanie knew her decisions hadn't always been the right ones, but she always knew Jesus loved her enough to help her over the rough spots. He had kept them safe despite her foolish pride that had kept her from forgiving. From admitting her own fault.

Jesus loved her.

Her parents loved her.

Jason loved her, too.

Melanie grabbed her dad's hand at the same time she flipped her palm up and clutched her mom's. Nine years of bitterness and hurt flowed out from her heart. Nine years lost.

"I love you." She barely uttered the words for the lump lodged in her throat.

"We love you too, baby." Her dad pulled her into his embrace. "Please forgive us."

All she could do was nod. She hugged him hard, fresh tears pouring from her eyes as she breathed his familiar scent. Her mother came up behind her and wrapped her arms around her. They huddled around the table with the healing power of tears flowing freely.

Go. A soft breeze blew in through the cabin from an open window.

Melanie sniffed and frowned. Go where? Go home? Go with her folks? Nothing made much sense, yet everything mattered.

Go. She looked up at her mom.

"Come home with us."

Go.

Melanie pushed back from the table. "I have to go. Can you watch Jason? I'll be right back."

She grabbed a handful of napkins for her nose and shot out the door, running down the path as fast as she could go.

Chapter Twenty

People milled around the open field as trucks backed up and loaded animals. Melanie smiled. The barbecue over, the auction a success.

And she'd missed it all.

She jogged along the fence to the gate and followed the path to the ranch-house kitchen. The door stood open, and voices filtered from the back of the house. In a bedroom with forest green walls, white trim and plaid curtains lay Gabe in a huge pine-framed bed surrounded by familiar faces.

"Hey, you. We were wondering how Bud came out of the scuffle." Gabe grinned, his eye turning black and a wide bruise marked his cheek. "Is he okay?"

"A little rattled, but he'll live to tell the tallest tale of any of his friends." She smiled back at Gabe. "How are you?"

"Little banged up. Nothing to worry about."

Jennifer bent toward her. "Pulled muscles, bruised back and probably a cracked rib. But he'll live. Dad said his lungs are clear and all the fingers and toes move." She grinned. "You can't keep ornery down. Lucky for him that bull was polled and never stepped on him."

"Ha." Gabe coughed. "I could take down a dozen bulls."

"Let's leave the bulls to Nick, okay?" Grace scolded. "One crazy son in the family is all I need."

"So, did we scare the living daylights out of your parents?" Martin sat in a chair beside a beautifully carved dresser. "Are they ready to run back to the city?"

Her new friends surrounded the bed of her fallen hero. She locked on Gabe, his dimple still evident even through the bruising. He'd risked his life for her son. "Thanks doesn't say enough, Gabe. I know Jason wouldn't be alive if not for you."

His eyes darkened. "I wouldn't let anything happen to Jason. None of us would."

Exactly. Dad was right. Curiosity drove Jason. What if someone wasn't around next time? What if someone got hurt, or worse? No, a working ranch was no place for an adventurous, curious eight-year-old boy. "God bless you all. Jason and I will be leaving in the morning with my parents. I just wanted to see how Gabe was holding up and tell you what a wonderful few weeks this has been. Thank you."

"Melanie, how about—" Gabe began.

"Your parents are going to love Jason. And it's a good idea he spends time with them. Get to know them. They are his grandparents." Grace offered a kind smile and a hug. "Make your peace. You all deserve it."

Her shoulders relaxed. "I wouldn't have realized it was time without you."

"Melanie," Gabe began again. He looked at his parents and they looked at him. Silence hung in the air for the stretch of a long second.

"Jennifer, could you help me a second?" Grace motioned toward the door. "Martin and I have some stuff left over that needs to go."

Martin frowned at his wife. "What stuff?"

"Just come with me. Let's go give Jen the box of leftover

pie for her dad." She held out her hand and he grasped it. "Melanie, come back and visit us soon."

"Oh." Martin winked at Melanie. "It's always a good time for pie. Yes, come back soon."

As they filed out the door, Melanie couldn't help but chuckle. "Subtle."

"As a freight train." Gabe lifted his fingers, the longing in his brown eyes obvious.

She stepped up beside the bed and took his hand. He grasped hers tight. "We're going to miss you."

Gabe stared at her. "We're?"

"You know Jason thinks you hang the stars. He'll be talking about nothing but you and the ranch for months."

His thumb moved over her wrist. "Jason?"

"I'll miss all of you."

"All of us?"

She bit her lip and frowned, her thumb returning the caress on the top of his hand. His skin was so warm, rough. So real. "You. I'm going to miss you, Gabe."

"Don't go."

She stared at the gash across his thumb. His suntanned arm now pale and covered with bruises. His fingers tightened around hers.

"Melanie. I don't want you to leave." The warm knuckle of his other hand urged her chin up. Moisture glistened in his deep, brown eyes. "Please stay."

Her heart leapt in response, yet what was the answer? Just a couple days ago, she didn't have a clue what to do with her life. Now she'd been given a second chance for an interview for a great job, her family restored, and the man she'd fallen in love with asking her to stay.

It was all too much, too soon.

"I can't," she whispered.

Silence hung thick. He squeezed her fingers and nodded.

"Your truck is in the barn." His gravelly voice tore at her heart. "The gate is always open."

"I'll remember that." Not trusting to say anything else, she let go of his hand and hurried from the room. She slipped down the hallway and out the back office.

She grabbed her keys off the wall before she closed the door.

The crisp scent of cool evenings tinged the air as golden-leafed aspen trees dotted the slopes. Bales of hay sat stacked in meadows. Herds of antelope bolted across freshly cut fields to scavenge all they could before the snow flew.

Gabe wandered along the path leading to the river. He protected his tender ribs against the boughs of the scruff pine in his way. He'd done his share of haying and mending fence. He'd wandered about and watched the grass grow. Funny how slowly time moved. By this time most years, he'd wake up one day to discover summer gone. All he'd done over the last weeks was wake up and dread another long day.

The path ended at the river. He followed the bank, knowing he'd end up at the jut in the river—the place where Jason had caught his fish. Gabe had experienced many happy times here on the river, but that afternoon ranked the best. As he drew closer, he saw his dad sitting on a broad rock.

"Catch anything?" He took a seat on a fallen log beside Martin.

"Nope, not even trying." Martin looked up and down the river. "Just came here to sit and think."

As his dad studied the water, Gabe noticed the stoop to his back and gray about his temples. Dad had always been larger than life. Since his heart attack, he'd slowed down. Gabe grabbed a pebble off the ground and whipped it into the water.

His dad looked real, vulnerable.

"Time to start thinking about culling timber and cutting

firewood for the winter. I'll go into town and have the blade on the log splitter sharpened."

"Uh-huh." Martin nodded.

"With all the extra livestock gone, we'll be able to bring the cattle in and take them down the canyon to winter."

"You've done a good job with this ranch, Gabe," Martin broke in, as he continued to look out over the water. "You've had good ideas for changes. The Circle D is in a good place."

Gabe stared at the back of his dad's head. He'd waited so long to hear a word of praise from his father. Now, he didn't know what to say.

"When my granddad homesteaded this land, he fought God and nature every step of the way to give the rest of us a good home. We moved rocks, strung fence, built a home. None of my brothers wanted to stay. I never wanted to leave. Lucky for me, your mom liked it up here, too."

Melanie's laugh echoed through his head. Gabe shook away the memory, only to have her smile float about in its place. He rubbed his fingertips together, the feel of her hand ingrained in his skin.

"The land gets in your blood. When you three boys were growing up, I always thought you'd be the one to stay."

God, the land, the community held Gabe in place. Where else would he go? Dad was right. He wanted to carry on tradition. He wanted to pass the Circle D down to the next generation of Davidsons. If there was a next generation. "I'm doing the best I can."

"Yes you are, son." Martin leaned back and faced Gabe, the lines in his face deeper, but the light in his eyes remained just as bright. "I'm glad you stayed."

The lump in this throat returned with a vengeance. "I'm glad, too."

Martin reached out and patted Gabe's thigh. The old man grinned. "The Scripture says there comes a time for a man to leave his mother and father and cling to a wife. What God joins together let no man pull asunder."

Dad had proposed to Mom on the ranch. As she told it, he chose the middle of a branding party to ask her to marry him. As he told it, all he did was ask her to wear his brand. He meant on her jacket; she thought forever. Who was he to argue?

Gabe shook his head. "Yeah, you and Mom have been a team ever since."

Still holding firmly to Gabe, Martin squeezed. "I ain't talkin' about me and Mom. I'm talkin' about you."

Gabe stilled. After a long moment, he looked over and his dad nailed him with a long, deep look, one he'd never before shared with his father.

"I had to drive clean to Pueblo to convince your mom I was the man for her." Martin never broke eye contact. "She's been worth every second we've shared together."

Gabe listened to the rush of water in the river. Soon the frost would settle and the ice would collect around the rocks. The winters in Hawk Ridge were long, cold and lonely.

"Gabriel, Ecclesiastics promises there's a time for everything. Is it your time?"

His time had come and gone weeks ago when he let Melanie leave. The biggest mistake of his life. He stood up. "I love you, Dad."

"I love you too, son."

The trek back up the path didn't take nearly as long as his careful descent to the river. Catching the angle of the sun, he estimated maybe an hour of light left in the day. No matter, he'd driven up and down the canyon since sitting in a baby seat. He'd find Melanie, and he'd find her tonight.

And he'd tell her he loved her.

As he pushed the last bough out of his way, he stopped dead in his tracks. A bright yellow pickup truck stood parked in front of the ranch house. Familiar voices filtered through the window and Fletcher barked at the door. Gabe took a cautious step, then another. Finally convinced it wasn't a dream, he strode across the lot as fast as his mending rib allowed.

The door opened and Fletcher bounded out, Jason Hunter on his heels. The dog had a Frisbee in his mouth, and no way was the boy going to get it. Grace stepped out, a smile as bright as the sun on her face.

Finally, Melanie came through the door. Dressed in jeans and a short-sleeved shirt, she looked like a tourist who'd lost her way. Gabe knew better. She was exactly where she should be.

She saw him. His stomach knotted as she stilled. A slow, wide smile spread across her face as she turned from Grace and started down the path through the yard toward him. They met at the front fender of her truck, the fender he'd fixed.

Gabe just stared at her.

"Aren't you going to say hi?"

"Hi."

A shadow crossed her face. Her eyes darted around the pens and sheds. "Um, is it all right for me to be here?"

A grin broke across his face and the pressure eased across his chest. "Yes, ma'am. Now I don't have to drive to Pueblo."

She tilted her head and frowned. "Pueblo?"

Shaking away her questions, he checked her over from head to foot. "What are you doing here?"

She waved a set of keys in the air. "Just picked up the keys from my landlord."

The keys to the first cabin on the path. Melanie and Jason's cabin. Blood rushed through his veins carrying anticipation he'd never felt before. "Landlord?"

Melanie closed the gap between them. She took him by the hand, her soft thumb caressing his stiff knuckles. He captured her slim fingers in his palm.

"When Jason and I left, we spent time with my mom and

dad. Broken bridges take time to mend, but we're on the right track. We drove to Montrose and I got the job."

His breath caught. "Melanie, I—"

She shook her head and placed her finger on his lips. "On the way home from Montrose, Jason and I got honest with ourselves. We didn't want to live there. So I talked to Mr. Leon about filling in for Shayna, and Jennifer asked if I could fill in for her at the clinic office while she's in Denver. School starts in about a week and Jason is enrolled."

Oh Lord...You've brought them back. Gabe didn't dare say a word. Colors came alive as he stared at her columbine blue eyes and rosy cheeks. The scent of lemons filled him, and all he wanted to do was bury his nose in her hair.

She waved the keys again. "I have a great cabin to live in until I find something else." Her smile dimmed as she kicked at a stone on the ground. "Jason and I were miserable." She looked up at him, her voice a stumble of hesitation. "Gabe, I was miserable. The city swallowed me whole. And I missed you something terrible."

He opened his arms and she stepped into his embrace. The hole in his life closed. Melanie filled him to overflowing. He ignored the pain in his ribs as he squeezed her close. "Missing you doesn't begin to describe it. When you left, I waited for the hurt to stop. It never did. It just became a big, black hole. Please don't leave again. I love you."

She rubbed her nose in his sleeve, the gesture releasing a flood of memories. He held his breath waiting for her response. They stood there, holding each other as the dusk grew around them.

Pushing back just far enough to meet his gaze, Melanie cleared her throat. "I was scared. If I left the security of my job, how would I take care of Jason? But then again, how could I stay when my heart wanted something else? I prayed like I'd never prayed before." Moisture misted her eyes as she smiled. "I love you, Gabe."

"I'm glad you came home." He lowered his head and touched her lips. Her arms tightened around his waist and she kissed him back, her lips warm and soft. Barking rang behind them. He lifted his head and saw Jason running up.

Gabe tucked Melanie close and waved at Jason. "Hey Bud, glad you came back."

Jason grinned and plowed into them with a big hug. "Mom said something about a Labor Day party. When's that gonna be?"

Epilogue

She couldn't eat another bite.

In the yard behind the church, the Labor Day picnic drew folks from all over the county. Ranchers and farmers talked harvest while the ladies arranged desserts on tables beneath the church eaves. Melanie sat at a table close to the toddler playground and waved to her boss, Elwood Leon. Great guy. Wanted her to take responsibility of the whole lawn and garden section of the store.

Jennifer came up and perched on the edge of the table. "I'll be back around Christmas. I don't think I'll have time off from class before that. I'll see if I can't bring Zac back with me for the holidays. I know Grace and Martin want to see him."

Melanie shot her a stern look. "Keep your mind on your studies. We're not sending you to school to lollygag."

"You fit in this town way too well. Hawk Ridge has swallowed you alive." Jennifer laughed. "Not to worry. I'm so not Zac's type."

Melanie wrinkled her nose. "Glad to hear it. I'll send you care packages."

Shayna moved into Melanie's sun and shaded her face at the same time placing a bundle in her arms. "Would you hold Adam while I fix a plate?"

"Just see if you can pry him away." Melanie drew the blanket back and smiled at the baby in her arms. Only a week old and already held by every man, woman and child in Hawk Ridge. "Stick with me, Adam. I'll split my ice cream with you."

"Thanks, Mel. RJ saved a place for me in line. C'mon, Jen, he's at the back of the line, so it's not like we're cutting in."

Jen beamed. She pushed from the table. "We'll be back."

They took off running toward the lanky cowboy who also decided to make Hawk Ridge his home. Melanie liked RJ. She thanked God for bringing dependable help for Gabe going into the winter months. He'd never admit it, but she knew Gabe appreciated the interest RJ took in the community. Gabe didn't trust drifters.

As if summoned by her thoughts, Gabe threaded through the crowd toward her, a strawberry cone in each hand. Would she ever get tired of watching that man walk? The lazy grin on his face warmed her clear down to her toes.

"Looks like you've found your niche." Gabe slid into place on the bench next to her. "Head babysitter, huh?"

"Kinda nice knowing I'm needed for something."

"I need you for a lot more than something."

He brushed a kiss over her lips. Melanie tasted strawberries, cream and adoration. A powerful combination by any standard. She nuzzled her nose into his neck. "I'm glad to hear it. I've grown kind of fond of you, too."

Gabe set the cones down and shifted beside her. He drew her back against his chest, his strong, suntanned arms wrapped around her. Goose bumps rose as his chin brushed against her ear. She cuddled Adam closer and watched Jason push Wyatt Deacon in the old tree swing across the yard.

Life couldn't get any better.

He tickled her ear with his lips. "Fond, huh? Would you say fond enough to marry me?"

She looked up at him and drank in his rugged profile, the

familiar sparkle in his root-beer-colored eyes. “That fond, and so much more.”

She kissed him to show how far beyond fond her love went.

Life had just become the best.

* * * * *

Dear Reader,

Don't you just love winning against all odds? I love happily-ever-after endings, which is the reason I write romance novels. When Gabe and Melanie first stormed my mind, I couldn't imagine how a stressed-out single mother from the big city and an overworked rancher from a small mountain town could ever set aside their worries and responsibilities long enough to let that spark of attraction ignite a coal, much less fan a flame. Melanie and Gabe didn't make time to search for soul mates for themselves. But God, who is faithful and just, brought them together at just the right time, just when they needed each other the most.

Isn't God great that way? Everyone wants to feel loved, cherished and appreciated. Sometimes God says yes, sometimes no. More often than not, He says wait. I have the hardest time with that answer. Don't we all? But if we're faithful with the little things, God will gift us with the best ones. Isn't that just too cool?

Thank you for choosing *Rocky Mountain Hero*, my debut novel. I hope you enjoyed Gabe, Melanie and Jason, and all the fine folks of Hawk Ridge. Remember, life's too short to dwell on the bad. Trust in the Lord. He has everything well in hand.

I would love to hear from you! Please visit my website www.audraharders.com or e-mail me at audraharders@yahoo.com. Or you can write to me c/o Steeple Hill Books, 233 Broadway, Suite 1001, New York, NY 10279.

Blessings to you!

Audra Harders

QUESTIONS FOR DISCUSSION

1. At the beginning of the book, Melanie is on her way to a job interview for a company she's not familiar with, in a town she's never visited. She wants to start her life anew. Do you ever feel like you want to leave the old behind and jump into something new? How do you feel about it?

2. Gabe takes his responsibility as manager of the family ranch to heart. He resents his brothers' having moved on with their lives and feels left behind. Is he justified in his feelings? What could he do besides allow the irritation to fester?

3. Gabe owns a video game system and invites Jason to play a game. Melanie had intended this vacation teach Jason the appeal of nonelectronic entertainment by enjoying the mountains and outdoors. Did Melanie choose the right approach to distract Jason? How would you distract a child from obsessive activity?

4. When Gabe receives the repair bill for Melanie's truck, he barters with her—he'll pay for the repairs if she plans the auction barbecue. Melanie feels helpless, thinking she has no choice but to accept Gabe's offer. Have you ever felt without choices in a serious situation? How did you handle it?

5. Melanie hadn't entered a church in years, blaming hypocrisy in the church when her friends abandoned her upon the discovery of her pregnancy. Has there been a time in your life where you've felt all alone in the world? How did you respond?

6. Grace Davidson has faith in the Lord to restore her splintered family. What drove the family apart?

7. Melanie is afraid Jason will injure himself on the swing despite the reassurances of the local folks that the swing is safe. She had to try it for herself before she could trust. Can you think of a circumstance where you didn't feel comfortable in a situation until you lived through it? How do you feel when people don't trust your opinion?

8. When Martin suffers a heart attack, Gabe realizes the vulnerability of his father and develops concern over his own ability to run the ranch without his father's ever-present advice. Do you fear the future? If you were in a similar situation and your mentor was leaving you, would you be confident in yourself to carry on? Why?

9. Jason is surrounded by love and acceptance from the Davidsons the moment they meet him. Melanie longs for that unconditional acceptance and love for her son. She secretly longs for it herself. Why would a person who desires love feel unworthy of being loved?

10. Grace Davidson loves to meddle in lives. She sees it as giving folks a helping hand. Gabe feels her involvement causes more harm than good. How do you feel about someone doing something for you without your permission because it's the best thing for you?

11. Melanie maintained contact with her parents, but for eight years never revealed she'd kept her son because they hadn't approved of her pregnancy. Do you think she should have mended fences long ago? How would you handle a situation like this?

12. Melanie falls in love with Gabe and senses he feels the same about her. Why would she want to leave the Circle D when everyone there and in the town of Hawk Ridge accepts and loves her? What would you do if you were in her situation?

13. What is Gabe's attitude after Melanie leaves? What difference do you think Melanie made in his life?

14. What kind of an impact did Gabe have on Jason's life? What did Gabe and Jason learn from each other?

15. Melanie and Jason live in Colorado Springs, a city with many economic and cultural opportunities. Yet Melanie wanted to raise Jason in a small rural town. Do you think she chose wisely?

Love Inspired™®

TITLES AVAILABLE NEXT MONTH

Available January 25, 2011

CHILD OF GRACE
Irene Hannon

THE PRODIGAL COMES HOME
Mirror Lake
Kathryn Springer

HOMETOWN DAD
Kellerville
Merrillee Whren

SEASON OF DREAMS
Jenna Mindel

HER VALENTINE FAMILY
Renee Andrews

SECOND CHANCE COURTSHIP
Glynna Kaye

LICNM0111

YES! Please send me 2 FREE Love Inspired® novels and my 2 FREE mystery gifts (gifts are worth about $10). After receiving them, if I don't wish to receive any more books, I can return the shipping statement marked "cancel." If I don't cancel, I will receive 6 brand-new novels every month and be billed just $4.24 per book in the U.S. or $4.74 per book in Canada. That's a saving of over 20% off the cover price. It's quite a bargain! Shipping and handling is just 50¢ per book.* I understand that accepting the 2 free books and gifts places me under no obligation to buy anything. I can always return a shipment and cancel at any time. Even if I never buy another book, the two free books and gifts are mine to keep forever.

105/305 IDN E7PP

Name (PLEASE PRINT)

Address Apt. #

City State/Prov. Zip/Postal Code

Signature (if under 18, a parent or guardian must sign)

Mail to Steeple Hill Reader Service:

IN U.S.A.: P.O. Box 1867, Buffalo, NY 14240-1867
IN CANADA: P.O. Box 609, Fort Erie, Ontario L2A 5X3

Not valid for current subscribers to Love Inspired books.

Want to try two free books from another series?
Call 1-800-873-8635 or visit www.morefreebooks.com.

* Terms and prices subject to change without notice. Prices do not include applicable taxes. N.Y. residents add applicable sales tax. Canadian residents will be charged applicable provincial taxes and GST. Offer not valid in Quebec. This offer is limited to one order per household. All orders subject to approval. Credit or debit balances in a customer's account(s) may be offset by any other outstanding balance owed by or to the customer. Please allow 4 to 6 weeks for delivery. Offer available while quantities last.

Your Privacy: Steeple Hill Books is committed to protecting your privacy. Our Privacy Policy is available online at www.SteepleHill.com or upon request from the Reader Service. From time to time we make our lists of customers available to reputable third parties who may have a product or service of interest to you. If you would prefer we not share your name and address, please check here. ☐

Help us get it right—We strive for accurate, respectful and relevant communications. To clarify or modify your communication preferences, visit us at www.ReaderService.com/consumerschoice.

LIREG10R

Enjoy a sneak peek at Valerie Hansen's adventurous historical-romance novel RESCUING THE HEIRESS, available February, only from Love Inspired Historical

"I think your profession is most honorable."

One more quick glance showed him that Tess was smiling, and it was all he could do to keep from breaking into a face-splitting grin at her praise. There was something impish yet charming about the banker's daughter. Always had been, if he were totally honest with himself.

Someday, Michael vowed silently, he would find a suitable woman with a spirit like Tess's and give her a proper courting. He had no chance with Tess herself, of course. That went without saying. Still, she couldn't be the only appealing lass in San Francisco. Besides, most men waited to wed until they could properly look after a wife and family.

If he'd been a rich man's son instead of the offspring of a lowly sailor, however, perhaps he'd have shown a personal interest in Miss Clark or one of her socialite friends already.

Would he really have? he asked himself. He doubted it. There was a part of Michael that was repelled by the affectations of the wealthy, by the way they lorded it over the likes of him and his widowed mother. He knew Tess couldn't help that she'd been born into a life of luxury, yet he still found her background off-putting.

Which is just as well, he reminded himself. It was bad enough that they were likely to be seen out and about on this particular evening. If the maid Annie Dugan hadn't been along as a chaperone, he knew their time together could, if misinterpreted, lead to his ruination. His career with the fire department depended upon a sterling reputation as well as a

SHLIHEXP0211

Spartan lifestyle and strong work ethic.

Michael had labored too long and hard to let anything spoil his pending promotion to captain. He set his jaw and grasped the reins of the carriage more tightly. Not even the prettiest, smartest, most persuasive girl in San Francisco was going to get away with doing that.

He sighed, realizing that Miss Tess Clark fit that description to a T.

You won't be able to put down the rest of
Tess and Michael's romantic love story,
available in February 2011,
only from Love Inspired Historical.

Copyright © 2011 by Valerie Whisenand

SHLIHEXP0211

After discovering her boss's dead body, Susanna Trent starts receiving strange packages, anonymous phone calls and thinly veiled threats. Worried for her life, Susanna must trust the only man who can help—wealthy executive Jack Townsend. As they work together, Jack and Susanna must overcome life-or-death stakes!

A DEADLY GAME

by VIRGINIA SMITH

Available February wherever books are sold.

www.SteepleHill.com

LIS44428

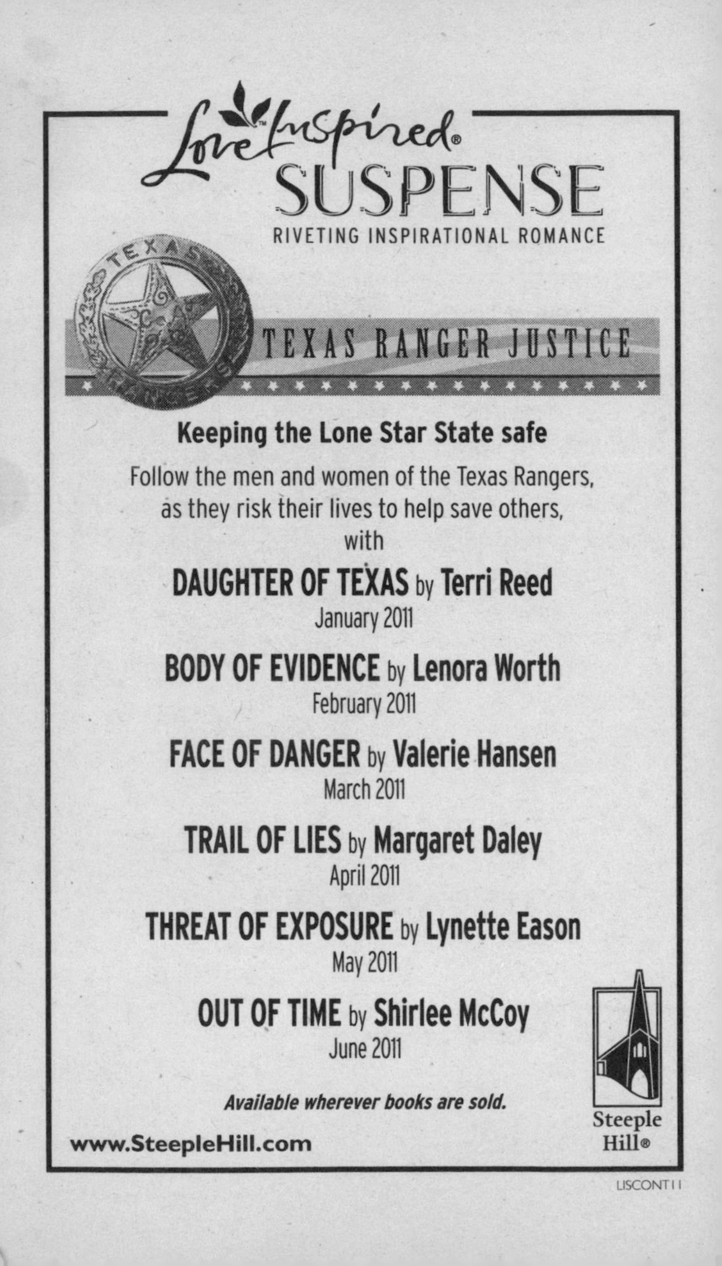
Love Inspired®
SUSPENSE
RIVETING INSPIRATIONAL ROMANCE
TEXAS RANGER JUSTICE
Keeping the Lone Star State safe
Follow the men and women of the Texas Rangers,
as they risk their lives to help save others,
with
DAUGHTER OF TEXAS by Terri Reed
January 2011
BODY OF EVIDENCE by Lenora Worth
February 2011
FACE OF DANGER by Valerie Hansen
March 2011
TRAIL OF LIES by Margaret Daley
April 2011
THREAT OF EXPOSURE by Lynette Eason
May 2011
OUT OF TIME by Shirlee McCoy
June 2011
Available wherever books are sold.
www.SteepleHill.com
Steeple Hill®
LISCONT11